Brett didn't know why he continued to hold Caitlin close, why he wasn't ready to let her go.

The silk of her hair lay soft against his cheek, and without a conscious thought, his lips brushed the strands in a whisper-soft kiss that was too out of line for anyone's good.

Her arms still locked around his neck, she lifted her face. A vibrant aquamarine gaze wrapped around him like seaweed in the surf.

His heart slammed into his chest.

Should he apologize? Make some moronic excuse for letting a hug get out of hand?

He tried to think of an apology, an excuse, some explanation of why his body had taken charge of his brain—until he spotted desire brewing in her eyes. And in the scheme of things, reason and good sense no longer seemed to matter.

So he lowered his mouth to hers....

Dear Reader,

We're deep into spring, and the season and romance always seem synonymous to me. So why not let your reading reflect that? Start with Sherryl Woods's next book in THE ROSE COTTAGE SISTERS miniseries, *The Laws of Attraction*. This time it's Ashley's turn to find love at the cottage—which the hotshot attorney promptly does, with a man who appears totally different from the cutthroat lawyers she usually associates with. But you know what they say about appearances....

Karen Rose Smith's *Cabin Fever* is the next book in our MONTANA MAVERICKS: GOLD RUSH GROOMS continuity, in which a handsome playboy and his beautiful secretary are hired to investigate the mine ownership issue. But they're snowbound in a cabin...and work can only kill so much time! And in *Lori's Little Secret* by Christine Rimmer, the next of her BRAVO FAMILY TIES stories, a young woman who was always the shy twin has a big secret (two, actually): seven years ago she pretended to be her more outgoing sister—which resulted in a night of passion and a baby, now child. And said child's father is back in town... Judy Duarte offers another of her BAYSIDE BACHELORS, in *Worth Fighting For,* in which a single adoptive mother—with the help of her handsome neighbor, who's dealing with a loss of his own—grapples with the possibility of losing her child. In Elizabeth Harbison's hilarious new novel, a young woman who wonders how to get her man finds help in a book entitled, well, *How To Get Your Man*. But she's a bit confused about which man she really wants to get! And in *His Baby to Love* by Karen Sandler, a long-recovered alcoholic needs to deal with her unexpected pregnancy, so she gratefully accepts her friend's offer of her chalet for the weekend. But she gets an unexpected roommate—the one man who'd pointed her toward recovery...and now has some recovering of his own to do.

So enjoy, and we'll see you next month, when things once again start to heat up, in Silhouette Special Edition!

Sincerely yours,

Gail Chasan
Senior Editor

Please address questions and book requests to:
Silhouette Reader Service
U.S.: 3010 Walden Ave., P.O. Box 1325, Buffalo, NY 14269
Canadian: P.O. Box 609, Fort Erie, Ont. L2A 5X3

WORTH FIGHTING FOR

JUDY DUARTE

Silhouette

SPECIAL EDITION®

Published by Silhouette Books

America's Publisher of Contemporary Romance

To Patricia Kawano Barberio, with whom I've shared laughter, tears and wine while we discussed— and sometimes cussed—life's unexpected curves. Together, we always come out on top.

I love you, Patty!

SILHOUETTE BOOKS

ISBN 0-373-24684-6

WORTH FIGHTING FOR

Copyright © 2005 by Judy Duarte

Visit Silhouette Books at www.eHarlequin.com

Printed in U.S.A.

JUDY DUARTE

An avid reader who enjoys a happy ending, Judy Duarte always wanted to write books of her own. One day she decided to make that dream come true. Five years and six manuscripts later, she sold her first book to Silhouette Special Edition.

Her unpublished stories have won the Emily and the Orange Rose, and in 2001, she became a double Golden Heart finalist. Judy credits her success to Romance Writers of America and two wonderful critique partners, Sheri WhiteFeather and Crystal Green, both of whom write for Silhouette.

At times, when a stubborn hero and a headstrong heroine claim her undivided attention, she and her family are thankful for fast food, pizza delivery and video games. When she's not at the keyboard or in a Walter Mitty–type world, she enjoys traveling, spending romantic evenings with her personal hero and playing board games with her kids.

Judy lives in Southern California and loves to hear from her readers. You may write to her at: P.O. Box 498, San Luis Rey, CA 92068-0498. You can also visit her Web site at www.judyduarte.com.

From the *Bayside Banner*:

A drive-by shooting on Saturday evening claimed the life of an eighteen-year-old pregnant woman at a downtown bus stop. The woman was rushed to Oceana General, where she was placed on life support until her baby girl was delivered by Caesarean section.

Kay Logan, a member of the board of directors of Lydia House, a nonprofit organization that helps homeless young women get their lives on track, said, "Jennifer Harper was once a teen runaway from the Midwest and was living on the street when she first came to Lydia House. She was well on her way to becoming a success story until this senseless tragedy occurred."

According to Mrs. Logan, funeral services for the single mother will be held at 2:00 p.m. this Saturday at the Bayside Community Church.

A hospital spokesman reported the five-pound two-ounce newborn was doing well and would be placed in foster care.

Chapter One

Lieutenant Brett Tanner had never done anything so stupid.

Not since he joined the U.S. Navy ten years ago.

And he damn sure didn't know why he did it now, after all this time. Curiosity, he supposed, but for some reason he felt compelled to drive by the house, to peer from a safe distance. To make sure his kid was okay.

He rode his black Harley Softail past the high school, where he'd first met Kelly, his son's mother, and turned left at the fire station. The old neighborhood appeared the same, but he knew better.

The bike made another left onto Periwinkle Lane, as though it didn't need a rider, then slowed to a stop.

Brett cut the engine before he reached the cul-de-sac, where the two-story house stood in silent testimony of the things that had remained the same.

And the things that hadn't.

The outside walls boasted creamy-white stucco. And the wood trim was painted a pale teal—something Kelly had repeatedly told him had needed to be done. Something he'd never gotten around to, since he'd been deployed most of the short time they'd been together.

The grass, obviously fertilized, was a deep shade of green and had been newly mown, the edges cut straight. A rainbow spray of flowers grew along the sidewalk—from the front porch to the drive, where a late-model, white Chevy pickup and a blue minivan rested.

For a moment, he had a masochistic urge to leave the Harley parked at the curb and saunter up the walk like he still owned the place.

But he remained rooted to the spot.

On a couple occasions he'd reconsidered his decision to walk away from his son without a fight. But that was only after having one too many beers. When he was thinking clearly, he knew he'd done the right thing.

His son, a little boy Brett hadn't seen since he was two, deserved to be happy.

Why confuse the poor kid and screw him up now? Too much time had passed, and David Hopkins was the only dad Justin had ever known.

Besides, with the duty Brett pulled, he'd be in and out of the kid's life like he was pushing through a revolving door. What good was that?

Brett didn't know how long he studied the house, the new fence, the bright yellow swing set in the backyard. But he stood there long enough to see that it was just the kind of home every kid ought to have.

One of those purple-flowered trees Kelly had always liked now grew in the front yard. A bright blue flag, adorned with a picture of a birdhouse, hung from the porch overhang, and a wrought iron bench with a floral seat cushion sat by the front door, where a wooden welcome sign hung.

It was vivid proof of all that was right in Kelly's world—now that Brett was no longer a part of it.

The relationship had been wrong from the get-go, he supposed. They'd squabbled about most everything. But when Kelly got pregnant, he'd insisted they get married for the kid's sake. And when she'd reconnected with her old boyfriend, he'd wanted an amicable split for the same reason.

So Brett joined the ranks of absent fathers. But at least he wasn't a deadbeat dad. The Navy deducted an allotment from his pay for child support. And each month he sent Kelly a personal check for an extra two hundred dollars—for incidentals. Stuff his kid might need. Something a dad ought to provide.

It was also a way to keep in touch, to let Kelly know where he was—in case his son needed him. In case she wanted to send him a picture or something.

She hadn't sent him squat, not even a thank-you. But he hadn't pressed her, even though something deep inside fought his passive reaction.

Instead, he'd taken out an additional $250,000

life insurance policy—above and beyond what the Navy would provide his son—should something happen to him.

It had been his way of doing right by the kid he'd fathered.

And so had his letting go, staying away and allowing his child to grow up in a loving, peaceful home. Little Justin had two parents to raise him, two people who could be civil to one another. It was bound to be a hell of a lot better childhood than Brett had suffered through.

Just then, a little boy wearing a pair of jeans, a white T-shirt and a red baseball cap came out of the neighbor's side yard. He ran a short distance down the sidewalk, leaped over a small hedge in the front of the house Brett had been watching, then dashed inside yelling, "Mom, I'm home."

That was his son. Justin.

Emotion clogged his throat, and his eyes went misty at the thought of what he'd given up.

But Justin was better off this way. Happy and settled in a home where two parents loved him. But that didn't mean the decision wasn't tearing Brett up inside.

Justin had been only four months old when Kelly told Brett she wanted to end their marriage, that she'd hooked up with her old boyfriend from college.

Brett's first thought was to tell her to give Justin to him and get the hell out of his life, but he'd managed a calm tone and used all the tact he could muster.

"What about the baby?" he'd asked her, when she

told him over the phone that things weren't working between them and she wanted a divorce.

"What about the baby?"

"I thought maybe I should raise him, since you and David probably want to have a family of your own."

"I'm Justin's mother," Kelly had cried into the telephone. "I'm not giving him up. He needs me, not a dad who's never home."

A sense of anger, frustration and hostility had come over him, making him want to fight her for his son. And he didn't like it. Didn't like what it meant, what he knew it would lead to, so he'd shut up, stepped back and let go.

Besides, what would Brett have done with the baby? Take him away from his mother? No way. Kelly loved the child. He knew that.

Visitation had been established through the uncontested divorce, and Brett had seen his son from time to time, but because of his military career, it wasn't very often.

With Kelly and her new husband always present, things had been awkward. But on the last visit, when Justin was two, the toddler had acted kind of timid. Kelly had said that Brett's presence was confusing him.

Maybe so, because Brett felt uneasy around his son, too. Hell, with his unstable upbringing, he didn't feel nearly as qualified to father his son as David was. The guy was a schoolteacher, for God's sake. So Brett had stepped back.

It hadn't been easy, and a couple of years ago, when Justin had gotten older, he'd contemplated stepping in and insisting Kelly tell the boy David wasn't his real dad. But Brett was afraid that would only screw the kid up and make him a hellion, like Brett had once been.

So he'd sucked it up and made the biggest sacrifice he would ever make. And time hadn't done a damn thing about easing the grief.

The same familiar ache settled deep in his chest, and his eyes began to water. Damn. He felt like bawling. And he hadn't cried in years. Not after he'd grown battle weary and lashed out at his warring parents in a fit of rebellion that damn near landed him in jail.

Brett started the engine and turned the Harley around. It was time to head back to Bayside. Back to the condo he was house-sitting for a Navy buddy. Back to a big-screen TV, a fridge full of beer and a crotchety old cat named Fred.

But his mind would remain on the vision he'd seen, the perfect life Kelly had created for his son.

His parents' nasty divorce and vicious custody battle had lasted most of his growing-up years and done a real number on him. For that reason, he'd sworn never to do that to a child of his own.

"I'd walk away first," he'd told Kelly, "rather than make my son a pawn, make him suffer like I did."

And Brett had kept his word—even though it nearly killed him not to be a part of Justin's life.

At the stop sign, he gunned the engine, then headed back to the condominium complex where he would spend his shore duty. But his chest still ached and his eyes stung.

What the hell was the matter with him?

Brett Tanner didn't cry. He sucked it up and did his duty. He did the right thing.

After all, he'd chosen the wrong road too many times in the past.

As tears welled in his eyes, he cursed the evidence of his weakness, then tried to shake the pain and anger as he sped through the city streets. He turned into the Ocean Breeze complex, just as a white Volvo appeared from nowhere.

A loud metallic thud sounded when his bike slammed into the car. His body flew through the air, then slid along the driveway.

He didn't feel any pain at first. Not until his head cleared and he felt the sting of asphalt on his knees and arm, followed by an agonizing ache where his shoulder had hit the ground first.

The impact had sent his two-hundred-dollar sunglasses flying, probably smashing them to smithereens.

How was he going to explain this to the other driver? Or to a police officer, if one showed up on the scene? Or to any of his buddies, if they ever caught wind of this?

He'd had his head up his ass, thinking about his son, about Kelly. About the raw pain in his chest and the tears that clouded his sight.

And he'd caused an accident.

A black shadow struck the car with a vengeance. Caitlin Rogers slammed on her brakes, but much too

late to avoid an accident. She threw the gearshift into Park, and glanced in her rearview mirror to see her
four-year-old daughter sitting wide-eyed in the car
seat in back.

"Baby, are you okay?"

Emily nodded. "What happened, Mommy?"

"I ran into someone. You wait here."

Caitlin swung open the door and rushed to check
on the motorcyclist she'd just struck.

Had she killed him? Maimed him? Oh, God.
Please let him be okay.

How could she have been so blind, so irresponsible?

She'd been so caught up in the trouble looming
over her that she'd been on autopilot and hadn't even
seen the motorcycle turn into the complex. All she'd
been thinking about these past few days was that she
might lose custody of the child she'd loved and
raised since birth, the precious little girl she hoped
to adopt.

Caitlin looked at the dazed man and saw a nasty
abrasion on his chin, a blood-speckled white T-shirt,
a scraped leather aviator jacket, jeans that were torn
and bloody at the knee. "I'm so sorry. I didn't see
you. Are you all right?"

"I'm fine."

The man slowly got to his feet, and she had to tilt
her chin to look him in the eyes—glassy blue eyes
that looked watery. Gosh, had she hurt him that badly? Had his injuries made him teary-eyed?

"It's all my fault," she said. "But I have insurance."

He grimaced and rubbed his shoulder. "Didn't

anyone ever tell you not to admit blame in a traffic accident?"

"No. But I was thinking about something else and not paying attention. I'm really sorry."

"Don't worry about it." He glanced at the raw and bloodied knuckles of his right hand. Then he looked at the scraped and battered bike, the dented gas tank, the broken mirror, the bent handlebars, the scratched leather seat that looked like a fancy saddle. He clicked his tongue, blew out a ragged sigh and rolled his eyes.

Gosh, she felt terrible about this. Thank God he was wearing a helmet. "Are you sure you're all right?"

"I'm fine. Really." He limped to the big, black motorcycle that lay on its side, then shut off the engine.

He didn't appear fine. But Caitlin had a feeling he'd looked pretty sharp on that bike before she ran into him.

Was that a Harley? Those things were expensive. And her insurance rates would probably skyrocket at a time when she needed every cent she could find.

She eased closer, and he looked up at her with the most incredible sky-blue eyes she'd ever seen. He had a scar over his right brow that made him look manly. Rugged. Not afraid of a fight.

Was she crazy? Maybe she'd hit her head on the steering wheel or something. What provoked her to gawk at the good-looking stranger like a star-struck teenybopper?

He looked at his mangled bike, grimaced and shook his head.

"I'm really sorry," she said again, the words sounding useless.

"Don't be." He caught her eye, drew her deep into his gaze. "Just for the record, the accident was my fault."

"I'll call the police," she said, as she turned and walked back to the car for her cell phone.

"Wait." He reached out, caught her by the arm and turned her around to face him. "It's no big deal. Let's not bother filing an accident report. I'll just pay you for the damages to your car."

She needed to watch her expenses, since she expected some hefty legal bills soon. Lawyers were expensive, and she intended to retain the best one she could find—even if it cost her every last dollar she'd saved. Because, if Caitlin wouldn't fight for her daughter, who would?

The system?

No way. Caitlin knew better than that.

For that reason, she ought to quit struggling with her conscience and let him take the blame for something that felt like her fault. But the brawny biker looked so vulnerable, so hurt.

"Maybe you should see a doctor," she said.

He offered a wry, one-sided grin, then gazed at her with wounded eyes. "I only hurt my pride. That's all."

Then he looked at her—really looked, as though assessing her for injury.

Or was he checking her out in a male/female sort of way? It had been so long since she'd dated that she'd nearly forgotten what that sensual, I'm-avail-able-and-interested eye contact felt like.

"Are you hurt?" he asked her.

Okay. So there went her romantic assumption. But that was just as well. Getting involved with any-one right now wouldn't be in her best interests. Or Emily's.

"I'm just a little shaky." She glanced at the car and saw her daughter peering out the driver's door with a look of awe on her face.

"My mommy can fix your owies," Emily said. "She's a nurse. And she has a whole bunch of Hello Kitty Band-Aids and the stuff that doesn't sting."

"Are you okay?" the man asked her daughter.

Emily nodded. "But you're bleeding really bad. Does it hurt?"

"No. Not a bit."

The wounded biker swiped a bloodied hand across his cheek, as though wiping something away. He left a red smear in its place.

"Are you crying?" Emily asked him.

"No. A bug flew in my eye."

Caitlin let his comment alone, since it appeased her daughter. But the man was obviously in pain. "You really ought to see a doctor."

"I don't want to see a doctor." Then he blew out a ragged breath and lifted the heavy bike. He tried to push it toward the carport, but the effort seemed to tax him. He checked something at the handle and near the pedal, then muttered—probably a swear word—under his breath.

Gosh. He was favoring that right leg.

"If you won't see a doctor, then come to my house and let me tend your wounds."

"That's not necessary." He continued toward the carport.

Caitlin had been on her way to the market, but she was too jittery to go now, so she turned the car around and returned to her parking space. She watched as the motorcyclist pushed his battered bike next to hers.

"Number 39 belongs to my neighbor, Greg Norse," she told him. "But he'll be gone for a while, so I'm sure it's all right if you leave the bike there."

"I know," he said. "Greg's a buddy of mine, and I'm house-sitting while he's in Australia for the next few weeks."

"Are you going to cat-sit, too?" Emily asked, as she climbed from the car with her favorite stuffed kitty in tow.

No one loved cats more than Emily. And Greg, bless his heart, let her come over and play with Fred whenever he was home.

"Yeah, I'm watching the dam—" He looked at her daughter, catching himself. "The darn cat."

"Fred is a good cat," Emily said in her furry friend's defense. "He's the best kitty in the whole world."

"I'm glad you think so," the biker said with an I'm-not-convinced smile. "That little beast is psycho."

"Maybe Fred doesn't like you," Emily said.

The biker smiled. "You've got that right."

"I wanted to baby-sit Fred," Emily told him, "but my mom is 'lergic to cats."

The biker glanced at Caitlin, then smiled at the child. "Maybe you can come over and feed him. He runs under the bed whenever I get close to him."

"Can I, Mommy? Please?" Emily's eyes held such longing, that Caitlin hated to tell the child no. But she didn't know this man very well.

"We'll see, honey." Then she extended a hand to the biker. "My name is Caitlin Rogers, and this is my daughter Emily. We live next door to Greg."

"Brett Tanner." He held up his battered hand. "I'm afraid we'd better shake after I get cleaned up."

"I'll show you where we live," Emily said eagerly.

The biker—or rather, Brett—took off his helmet, revealing chocolate-brown hair cut in a military style. He had a nice face, with baby-blue eyes and a classic, square-cut jaw. In fact, he was a good-looking man who probably had his share of female admirers.

"You were leaving," he said. "And that dent on your hood and grill looks bad, but your car ought to drive okay."

She smiled and held up a trembling hand for him to see. "The car's in better shape than my nerves. I'll wait for a while. Besides, I want to check you out." Warmth flooded her cheeks. "I mean, check your injuries."

"I know what you meant." He slid her a devilish grin that made her wonder what it would have been like to meet him under different circumstances.

But enough of that. Right now, Caitlin's only focus was Emily. And ensuring that the little girl's biological father didn't take the child away from the only mother she'd ever known.

"Come on," Caitlin said. "Let's get your wounds cleaned up."

Brett didn't know why he'd let Caitlin talk him into this. As he followed her to the house, he glanced at his bloody knuckles. Hell, this was nothing. He'd had worse scuffles as a teenaged delinquent—before Detective Harry Logan had taken an interest in him and helped an angry, surly seventeen-year-old get his life back on track.

So why had he agreed to let the petite blonde with sea-green eyes lead him into her house?

Because the nurse was one hell of an attractive lady, and he didn't mind letting her practice a little TLC. It had been a long time since a woman had fussed over him.

Besides, her kid was really cute. And a cat lover, no doubt. Maybe she could coax that crazy feline to eat, so Greg wouldn't come home and find out his good buddy had let the damn critter starve to death under the bed.

At the front door, which boasted a flowery wreath in colors of green, pink and lavender, the attractive blonde slipped a key into the deadbolt, turned the knob and let them inside.

Women sure liked to leave their mark on a place.

Inside, the house was neat and clean, although the furniture looked a bit worn. He caught of whiff of something fragrant. Potpourri?

His mom used to display crystal bowls full of that scented, shaved wood and dried flower petals throughout the house.

"The bathroom is this way," Caitlin said.

He followed her down the hall and into the guest bathroom, which had pale pink walls and a lacy white curtain. Floral-printed decorative towels hung on the racks and matched the shower curtain.

"Can I help?" Emily asked.

"No, honey. There isn't much room in here for three of us."

She had that right. The walls seemed to close in on them the minute he'd stepped inside with her, making him even more aware of their difference in height. And their gender.

As she bent to retrieve something from under the sink, he couldn't help but appreciate the gentle curve of her hips, the way the white fabric fit a nicely shaped bottom. She straightened and set a first-aid kit on the countertop.

"I can do this myself," he said, feeling a bit awkward and vulnerable.

"Don't be silly. I insist." She took his bad hand in hers, gripping it with gentle fingers that sent a flood of warmth coursing through his blood.

Inside the tight quarters, he caught a whiff of her scent, something alluring and tropical.

While she worked on washing the grit and asphalt from his knuckles, he couldn't help but assess her with an appreciative eye.

She wore a pair of white pants cropped at the calf. And a lime-green T-shirt that probably would reveal the midriff of a taller woman, but the hem merely tickled her waistline.

Did she have a husband?

He didn't see a ring on her hand. But that didn't mean much. Kelly had taken off her wedding band while he'd been in the Middle East.

The water and antibacterial soap stung, but her ministrations were gentle, thorough. Professional. Yet his thoughts weren't those of a patient. Or a neighbor.

"Are you married?" he asked, unable to quell the curiosity.

Her movements slowed, but quickly resumed without her looking up. "No, I'm not."

Divorced then, since she had a kid.

"Mommy," Emily said from the doorway. "Can I get Brett a Popsicle?"

"You can't reach the freezer door. And he might not want one," the mother said.

"I can push a chair to the fridge. Then I can reach it." The little girl offered him a bright-eyed grin. "Do you want a Popsicle? That's what my mommy gives me after I get my owie bandaged."

"Thanks for the offer, but I'm afraid a Popsicle will ruin my appetite for dinner." Brett wasn't used to kids, but he figured her mother would appreciate his thoughtfulness.

"What are you having for dinner?" Emily asked.

"I'm going to drive through one of those burger joints." Whoops. Driving wasn't an option until he got his Harley fixed. He chuckled, then added, "I guess I'll have to walk, though."

"Want to have dinner with us?" Emily asked. "We're having spusghetti."

Actually, he liked Italian food and wondered if Caitlin was a good cook. Probably. She seemed to have domestic stuff down pat. "Thanks for asking, Emily. But I'll probably just rustle up something to eat from the pantry."

At least, he hoped so. He'd come in late last night, and Greg hadn't left him much to choose from by way of food in the fridge. And with his bike out of commission for a while...

"What does rustle up mean?" Emily asked.

"It means find something."

"Greg never buys food, 'cept for Fred. That's why he goes to Burger Bob's all the time... 'cept when he eats with us." The little girl offered him a sweet, expectant smile. "Spusghetti is better than those crunchy little brown fishies that Fred eats. I know, 'cause I tasted one once, and it was yucky."

Caitlin looked up from her work on his hand. "I still feel the accident was my fault, Brett. Please join us for dinner. It's the least I can do."

He ought to turn tail and run, get the heck out of Dodge. But for some reason, sharing *spusghetti* with his pretty neighbor and her little girl sounded kind of appealing.

"Are you sure it's no trouble?" he asked the mother.

"I'm sure. But Emily will probably expect you to play cards or a board game with her. That's the usual after-dinner routine when Greg comes over to eat."

"It's hard to believe a gruff guy like Greg plays kid games." Brett shook his head and grinned. His buddy stood about six-two and weighed more than two hundred pounds. And he was about as tough a man as the Navy had to offer.

Caitlin chuckled. "He plays a killer game of Candyland and Go Fish."

Greg? That mountain of a man who smoked cigars and could cuss a blue streak?

"Amazing." Brett realized he had something on his buddy now.

"Okay," Caitlin said. "Sit on the commode so I can look at your knee."

He wondered if she'd ask him to remove his pants. A part of him—that rebellious side he'd allowed to run amok during his youth—hoped she would.

"Do you mind if I cut your jeans?" she asked.

Score one for the lady. "Nah. Go ahead. They're going in the trash anyway."

She pulled scissors from the first-aid kit, then knelt at his feet and began to snip at the denim fabric. Her hair had white-gold highlights that probably lit up on a sunny day or in the candlelight.

He could imagine her walking hand in hand with a guy in the summer sun, sitting across a linen-draped table at a high-class restaurant.

What he couldn't imagine was her not having a man in her life.

What was the deal with her and Greg? Were they friends? Lovers?

And what about Emily's father? Where was he? And why had he let a woman like Caitlin slip away?

Brett wasn't sure why he was so curious about the

men in her life. It's not as though he wanted a shot at dating her himself. He made it a point to steer clear of women with kids.

But for now, he couldn't see any reason why he shouldn't join them for *spusghetti* and a game of Go Fish.

It beat the heck out of munching on dried cat food in front of the TV.

Chapter Two

Brett stood before the woven, heart-shaped welcome mat on his pretty neighbor's front porch and glanced at his watch—five-fifty. Ten minutes early.

He paused before knocking.

What had he been thinking when he'd agreed to dinner? Should he try and figure out a way to back out graciously?

Unlike his buddy Greg, Brett wasn't into cats, board games or neighborly get-togethers.

And Caitlin was just the kind of woman he steered clear of—a homemaker, like Kelly had been. And probably just as set in her ways and disagreeable. But to make matters worse, Caitlin also had a kid—and an ex-husband, no doubt.

It was just the kind of broken household Brett didn't want to be a part of.

His stomach rumbled, urging him to put aside his reservations for the sake of hunger. He should have walked ten or twelve blocks to the twenty-four-hour convenience store on Vine, but he'd spent the better part of the afternoon on the telephone looking for a certified Harley repair shop.

He'd found one in Bayside, and the owner had come out to look over the battered bike about twenty minutes ago.

The estimate was astronomical, but not a surprise. Six months ago, Brett had paid over twenty grand for the new Softail. Then he'd put a fortune into the high-priced accessories he'd added, not to mention the custom paint job. So he had no other choice but to let the mechanic from Hog Specialists haul it back to the repair and body shop.

And since Greg had loaned his pickup to his brother, Brett was left without wheels until the bike was fixed. Damn. He wasn't about to spend his leave on foot, so he'd have to rent a car, which he'd probably do tomorrow. But for now, he was temporarily stranded.

So why should he back out and tell Caitlin he wasn't hungry when he was actually starving?

Just as he lifted his good hand to rap at the door, a movement near the window caused him to glance to the right, where Emily peered through the white slatted shutters.

She had the front door open before he knew it.

"How come you were just standing there for a long time? My mommy won't let me open the door unless someone knocks."

He scanned beyond the doorway, looking for her mother, hoping Caitlin wouldn't think he'd been waiting at the door trying to muster a little courage. Not seeing her, he lifted his bandaged knuckle, trying to sidetrack the child by reminding her that he had an injury. "It hurts to knock."

"Then you should have ringed the doorbell."

Smart kid. Too smart.

"Come in." Her smile lit up her face in a warm welcome.

She was a cutie, that's for sure. Her mom had pulled back the sides of her long, blond hair with brightly colored, kitty-cat barrettes and dressed her in a white top, pink-and-white striped shorts and little white sandals.

"Guess what?" Emily's eyes danced like sugar-plum fairies, and she answered before he could ponder her secret. "I got to butter the bread and shake the sprinkles on it."

"Your mom is lucky to have such a great helper," he said.

"I know." The little girl took him by his good hand and led him into the house.

He hadn't paid much attention to the decor when he'd come inside earlier, but he did now. The cozy living room had an overstuffed sofa with a floral print in shades of pink and green, an antique rocking chair by the hearth, framed photographs placed on light oak furniture and lots of girly doodads on the pale green walls.

"Mommy!" Emily cried. "He's here."

Brett's pulse rate slipped into overdrive, as he waited for Caitlin to respond—a visceral reaction he didn't want and hadn't expected. Heck, she was just a neighbor.

Okay, so she was nice to look at. And she had a gentle touch, a lilt in her voice. That didn't mean he was interested in her in a romantic sense. The single mom was too heavy-duty for him.

"Hi," Caitlin said, as she walked out of the kitchen wearing a yellow sundress and a breezy smile— a perfect blend of Suzy Homemaker, Florence Nightingale and Meg Ryan. "I didn't hear the bell."

"That's 'cause he didn't push the button," Emily interjected. "And his owies hurt too much, so he couldn't knock."

The heat in Brett's cheeks suggested he'd turned a brilliant shade of red, but he shrugged off the embarrassment and hid his discomfort behind a grin. "Emily spotted me through the shutters and opened the door before I got a chance to knock."

"Is your hand still bothering you?" Caitlin asked, nodding toward his bandage.

"Nah," he lied. "It's fine. The knee, too. I'm almost back to fighting weight."

As she took his wrist and assessed her handiwork, he couldn't help but study her. She had a light sprinkle of freckles across a slightly turned-up nose and dark, spiked lashes that were much longer and thicker than he remembered.

Standing this close, he caught a good whiff of her

perfume, or maybe it was body lotion. Piña colada? Or some other tropical drink? Whatever it was smelled darn good.

"I'm not sure what you did to this," she said, "but it's damp and coming undone."

A piece of tape had lifted, probably from the steam and spray of the shower he'd taken before walking over here. He had a feeling she would offer to redo it for him, and the thought of her fussing over him again didn't bother him nearly as much as it should have.

Brett's lifestyle wasn't conducive to family life or happy ever after. He loved the Navy and flying choppers too much to give them up. And even if he bit the bullet and gave marriage or a one-on-one relationship another try, he wouldn't look twice at a woman with kids. That kind of gig was built-in trouble and turmoil, as far as he was concerned. And it smacked of a future rife with disagreements, threats and family court.

No. All that baggage made Caitlin off-limits.

But, hey. What was a little hand holding while she tended his wounds? A man wouldn't mind being sick or injured, just to have a woman like her hover over him.

She tucked a golden strand of hair behind her ear, revealing a pearl earring and a slender neck made for nuzzling and kissing, then glanced up at him with expressive, oceanic eyes. "I'll get the first-aid kit, just as soon as I drain the spaghetti. It won't take long."

"Don't worry about it now," he said, knowing the TLC bit wasn't something he should encourage.

"You can just slap another piece of tape on it later. After dinner."

"It needs a whole new bandage, but I'll wait." Then she turned and walked back to the kitchen with a determined step.

"Is there something I can do to help?" Brett asked, his voice chasing after her.

"Not a thing," she hollered from the other room. "I'll have dinner on the table in no time at all."

"I already did all the helping," Emily told him with little-girl pride. "Want to see what else I did?"

Brett nodded. "Sure."

When Emily took his hand again, it did something sappy to him. Something that touched a part of him he'd kept hidden. A part of him that longed to connect to a child.

His child, of course.

But this particular kid, as cute and smart and precocious as she was, seemed to fit the ticket—for tonight, anyway.

He'd have to be careful, though, since the mother scared him.

All right. That wasn't entirely true. Caitlin didn't scare him at all. But his attraction to her left him a little unbalanced.

"See?" Emily said, pointing to the dining room table that had been set with plain, white everyday wear. Nothing fancy. No romantic touches to cause him to feel uneasy.

A water glass sat in the middle of the table, with three drooping daisies and a red blossom of some kind. And a child-sketched crayon drawing sat at each plate, indicating who sat where.

Brett smiled when he saw his place. Emily had spelled his name with a skinny *B*, no *R*, a leaning *E* and only one *T*. And she'd drawn his picture, adding a bandage on the stick man's face and hand.

"The table looks great," he told the little girl. "And so does the picture of me."

"You can have it when you go home. And then you can put it on the 'frigerator so Fred can see it."

"Sounds like a perfect place for such a special piece of art." He offered her a smile, but his mind drifted to his own son, a boy who wore a red baseball cap and leaped over small hedges with a single bound.

Had Justin made pictures like that when he was Emily's age? Did he like to color?

If so, did Kelly display the artwork on the refrigerator for all the world to see?

Brett figured she did.

Caitlin entered the dining room with oven mitts on both hands, carrying a bowl of spaghetti sauce. "Usually, I fill our plates in the kitchen. But I thought it might be best if we ate family style."

The family thing might be kind of nice, he supposed.

When Caitlin reached to set the sauce on the table, the neckline of her sundress gapped a bit, giving him a glimpse of white lace and the soft swell of her breast—just enough for his thoughts to drift in a direction that wasn't at all neighborly.

"I have a bottle of red wine," she said. "Would you like me to open it?"

"Sure. Why not?"

She smiled, then returned to the kitchen.

Five minutes later, they sat at the table—family style. It was a weird experience for Brett. Surreal, actually. But kind of interesting.

Caitlin fixed a plate for Emily, filling her glass with milk. Then she poured wine for herself and Brett.

He had half a notion to offer a toast. But to what? Friendship? Being temporary neighbors? An accident that, even before he paid to have her car fixed, would cost him nearly ten grand in parts, labor and bodywork, not to mention custom paint?

That didn't make sense. So, instead, he lifted the glass and took a drink, hoping to wash away an unwelcome attraction to the kind of woman who would complicate his life—if he let her.

Caitlin didn't know why she'd brought out that bottle of wine. Just trying to be a good hostess, she guessed. She'd been given a couple of bottles of Merlot in a gift basket during a hospital Christmas party a year or so ago. She'd offered to open one for Greg once, after he'd worked on the starter for her car. But he preferred beer, which she'd never acquired a taste for and didn't keep in the house, so they'd settled for iced tea.

Dinner progressed with little fanfare, but Emily seemed to latch on to Brett. It didn't seem to bother him, and he was good with the child. In fact, it appeared that he was enjoying the little-girl chatter as much as Greg did. Maybe more.

So Caitlin sat back and watched.

Emily sucked up a long strand of spaghetti, splattering a bit of marinara sauce on her chin, and studied their temporary neighbor. "How come you don't like Fred?"

Brett glanced at Caitlin as though he didn't know how to answer the child. Earlier, he'd referred to Fred as a psycho cat, so Caitlin assumed they'd had a run-in or two.

"Fred doesn't like me," he told her daughter. "And he hisses if I come near him."

"Maybe I need to tell him you're nice and he shouldn't be afraid of you," said Emily.

"Maybe so." Brett cast her a smile, then returned to his meal, twirling spaghetti onto his fork. His dark brow furrowed in concentration.

He was handsome, and if Caitlin didn't have enough complications in her life, she might strive to be more neighborly, more open to romance. As it was, she'd better steer clear of the man. She wasn't sure how the courts would look upon her having a boyfriend or dating. Her case would be based upon her providing a stable home and having a solid bond with the child she loved, a child who was the top priority in her life.

"Can we come over and visit Fred tomorrow?" Emily asked Brett.

It saddened Caitlin that she had to deny Emily a pet, just because of her allergies to dander. So she always let Emily visit the neighborhood cats and dogs whenever possible.

"I can't imagine Fred being fun to play with," Brett said, "but you can come over, if your mom wants to bring you."

When he looked at Caitlin, she nodded. Emily was especially partial to cats, the kind of animal that bothered Caitlin's allergies the most. The little girl also gravitated toward kind and gentle men, especially Greg, and Gerald Blackstone, the older man who lived next door.

Caitlin tried to tell herself it was because Emily was a loving child who liked people, especially people with pets. It seemed reasonable since Greg had a cat, and Gerald and his wife had Scruffy, a terrier-mix they let Caitlin and Emily take for daily walks. But sometimes Caitlin wondered whether not having a daddy made Emily draw close to any kind man who had time for her.

Emily did, of course, have a father, as much as Caitlin wished that wasn't the case.

He was alive and well in the Riverview Correctional Facility, awaiting release and wanting custody of the child he'd never seen. A child whose mother died from wounds received in a drive-by shooting.

The possibility of the court ordering Caitlin to relinquish Emily was almost unbearable to ponder. How could she possibly hand over her foster daughter to a man who'd been involved in an armed robbery that had left a man paralyzed? It was enough to make Caitlin ill, whenever she thought about it.

What would happen if the little girl who loved rainbows and kitties was uprooted from the only mother and home she'd ever known and turned over to a convicted felon?

Caitlin couldn't imagine. But she, better than anyone, could guess.

She'd spent the first few years of her life in the inner city of San Diego, oftentimes in homeless shelters run by the Salvation Army. Her mom, an on-again, off-again prostitute and drug addict, couldn't get her act together. And by the time Caitlin was seven, she'd entered the first of many foster homes.

By the age of eleven, she'd finally settled into a stable home—one she'd hoped would be her last. But before her twelfth birthday, her mother went into a court-ordered rehab that seemed to work. And when the woman came out, she wanted Caitlin back.

Caitlin had cried, begging her foster mom, as well as her caseworker, to do something. But her pleas went unheard. And in the end, no one spoke up on her behalf, no one cared enough to fight a system that tried its best to reunite parents and children.

A social worker was ordered to take her to a run-down apartment to live with a mother whose taste in men hadn't improved. Six months later, her mom's boyfriend came home drunk one night and beat her mother to death. It was the kind of thing Caitlin wouldn't want any child to witness.

She glanced at Emily and felt a fierce ache in her chest.

No, Caitlin wouldn't give up *her* foster daughter. Not without a fight.

After a pleasant dinner, Brett joined Caitlin in a game of Go Fish. He actually enjoyed playing with the child, even though he had to turn his back whenever she organized her cards by spreading them face up on the beige carpet.

At eight o'clock, Caitlin told Emily it was time for bed.

"Oh, Mommy. Please let me stay up longer. I'm not even tired." Her little-girl plea was enough to make Brett want to jump in and argue for one more game. But since Caitlin had a loving but firm smile fixed on her face, he figured it wouldn't be a good idea to buck the system.

"Tell Brett good night," Caitlin said.

The child got up from the spot where she'd been sitting on the living room floor, padded to the sofa, put her arms around Brett and gave him a pint-sized hug that damn near squeezed the heart right out of him. "Good night, Brett. Thank you for coming over to play with me."

Brett smiled, relishing the scent of childhood, ice-cream sundaes and daydreams. "Sleep tight, pumpkin."

As she turned to go, he added, "Don't let the bedbugs bite."

Emily stopped in her tracks and turned. "What are bedbugs?"

Oops. He hadn't meant to freak her out before bedtime, make her have nightmares about critters climbing in her bed. So he tapped his finger on the tip of her turned-up nose. "They're little cooties that like to sleep with naughty boys who don't take baths and don't mind their mothers."

Emily smiled, revealing two cute dimples. "Then they won't get in my bed."

"I'm sure they won't." He had the urge to give her another hug, but that felt a little too daddy-ish. And God knew he didn't want to step on anyone's toes.

"Did the bedbugs used to sleep with you when you were little?" she asked.

A smile tugged on his lips. "Not when I was your age." But if his cootie explanation held true, his bed would have been bombarded with them when he was a hell-bent teen.

"Okay, young lady. Off to bed." Caitlin took her daughter by the hand, then looked at Brett. "Excuse me. I'll be back in a couple of minutes."

He nodded, then watched them head down the hall, his focus on the pretty mother, on the sway of her hips, the way the hem of her dress brushed against shapely calves.

Now was a good time to leave, to thank her for dinner, then be on his way. But for some stupid reason, he waited on the living room sofa for her to return.

He scanned the room, spotting the framed photographs of Emily on the mantel and on various tables throughout the room. He snatched one from the lamp table to his right and studied the picture of a bald-headed baby with a bright-eyed smile and sparkling-clear dribble on her chin.

Without any hair, she kind of looked like Justin had, when he was a baby.

Had Kelly taken a ton of pictures and placed them throughout her house, too? Probably.

Brett put the photograph back, grabbed the deck of cards off the coffee table and began to shuffle them over and over, just for something to do.

When Caitlin returned, she took a seat in the easy chair that rested by the fireplace.

Good move. It saved them both from feeling awkward. Well, it had saved him, anyway. Caitlin hadn't given him much indication that she found him as attractive as he found her. And that was a good thing. It made keeping his distance easier.

"Do you have any idea how long your motorcycle will be out of commission?" she asked.

"Not long," he lied. The mechanic from Hog Specialists said it would take a month or so, since the parts had to be ordered and weren't always easy to get. But he didn't want Caitlin feeling any guiltier over that damned accident than she already appeared to. "I'll probably rent a car anyway."

A look of remorse settled over her pretty face, and he wanted to see it lift. The accident had been mostly his fault, no matter what she thought.

"I've been wanting to buy an SUV," he said, "so this is the perfect opportunity to try one out before I fork over the cash."

She nodded, then managed a half smile. "I'd be happy to give you a ride to the rental place, if you need one."

That would be great. He didn't like being grounded. And being stranded was even worse. "Maybe, if you have some free time, we could go tomorrow."

"I have to work in the afternoon, but I can take you in the morning."

"Thanks." He studied his motorcycle boots for a moment, thinking about how tough it must be to raise a kid alone, to have to worry about babysitting and child care. Then he looked up and caught her eye. "Who watches Emily for you, while you work?"

"Gerald and Mary Blackstone, the retired couple who live in the end unit. They've become surrogate grandparents."

He didn't know why he asked. Curiosity, he supposed. "What about her father?"

Caitlin paused, then blew out a whispery breath. "Emily doesn't know her father. He hasn't been a part of her life."

Brett sat up straight, suddenly interested in Caitlin's past. In the man who'd walked away from Emily.

It wasn't any of his business, and he shouldn't ask, but he wanted to know more. "Does he, Emily's dad, pay child support?" Somehow it mattered a lot. Brett wanted to know the man was doing right by the little girl and looking out for her the best way he knew how.

"No," Caitlin said. "He doesn't pay anything."

Brett couldn't leave it alone. "Does he contact her at all?"

"No." Caitlin stood and walked toward the window, looked out upon the darkened complex lit by Tiki-style lamps. "But he wants to."

"And that bothers you?" Something twisted in Brett's gut. He sensed trouble coming down the pike. Hadn't he experienced enough domestic squabbles of his own?

His mom and dad had spent years in court fighting over every damn thing imaginable, while their son got caught in the crossfire until he rebelled the only way an angry teenager knew how.

"Yes, it does bother me. The idea of her father popping into her life tears me up inside. She doesn't even know him."

Brett figured Kelly would probably feel the same way, if he contacted her now and said he wanted to have a relationship with Justin. Call it an experiment, but getting a handle on Caitlin's feelings seemed like a good way to gauge how things would pan out if he approached his ex.

Caitlin had grown quiet, solemn, as though she was still hurting from the divorce.

Or maybe from her ex-husband's desertion.

Like a hound closing in on a buried bone, Brett couldn't seem to let it go. "Maybe Emily's dad had a good reason for not sticking around."

Did it tear the man up inside to walk away from his kid, like it had Brett? Did he get an ache in his chest each time he saw a child about the same age as his own?

Brett had to stop beating himself up. According to Harry Logan, the retired detective who'd managed to stop Brett's downhill slide into the juvenile justice system, Justin was happy.

And if anyone knew what made a boy tick, it was the guy who'd helped a dozen or more delinquents get their lives back on track. A guy who'd put his heart where his mouth was, opening his arms, his home and his family to boys with nowhere else to turn. And Brett was happy to count himself as one of the bad-boys-turned-good-guys.

According to Harry, who'd done a little investigating, Justin's stepfather was good to him. Maybe not better than Brett would have been, but at least David was home every night and not deployed to the far side of the earth flying a Sea Hawk and risking his life.

Hell, as a Navy helicopter pilot, Brett was away the better part of the year. What kind of husband or father could he ever hope to be?

"So tell me about you," Caitlin said, doing them both a favor and diverting the conversation to something more pleasant. "How did you meet Greg?"

"We met during a bar fight at a seedy joint in downtown San Diego. And we've been watching each other's backs ever since."

"Greg was involved in a bar fight?" Her brows lifted and her eyes widened. "I can't imagine it. He's so sweet and gentle."

Were they talking about the same guy? That knockdown drag-out hadn't been the first for Greg, who became a superhero whenever he'd had too much to drink.

Brett grinned as the memory surfaced. "Greg saw a couple of the local boys harassing the female bartender and decided to step in and correct the situation."

"Now that sounds like the Greg I know."

Brett couldn't help but chuckle. "Yeah, well the lady bartender stood over six feet tall and had forearms the size of Popeye's. I might have been a bit snockered myself, but her afternoon shadow suggested she—or rather he—could hold his own."

"So Greg stepped in?"

"And about got his head knocked in with a chair, until I jumped in to help. And just as the fight turned into a rip-roaring free-for-all, the bartender pulled a gun and settled it."

"Was anyone shot?"

"Just the ceiling. But Greg and I limped out of there with our share of cuts and bruises. We've been buddies ever since."

She smiled, then glanced at his bad hand. "Speaking of cuts and bruises, I nearly forgot to fix that bandage for you. I'll be right back."

When she returned with the first-aid kit, she took a seat next to him on the sofa.

He caught a faint whiff of a tropical breeze, felt the sultry heat as she touched his arm. Was she feeling it, too? The attraction that seemed to grow stronger each time their gazes met?

As she removed the tape and gauze from his hand, her knee brushed against his thigh, sending a shimmy of heat through his blood. He watched her hair sweep along her shoulder and fought the urge to touch the golden strands, to see if they felt as silky as they looked.

Instead, as she rewrapped his hand and fastened

the tape, he tried to waylay the flicker of desire that taunted his better judgment. "Let me know what the bodywork on your car is going to cost."

"I'll take it in for an estimate, but I still feel as though that accident was my fault." She looked up from her work, then furrowed her brow when the scrape on his chin caught her eye. She probed around it lightly. Her soft, gentle fingers lingered on his jaw.

When she looked into his eyes, he was swept into that sea-blue gaze. Her tropical scent swirled around them, making him envision an evening luau for two on a deserted beach.

Something passed between them, something he suspected she'd felt, too. A need. A hunger.

He wouldn't act on it, although it damned near killed him not to. "Thanks."

"My pleasure," she said, her eyes still fixed on his.

He knew better than to reach out and touch her, but when she looked at him like that, with what seemed like virginal interest, his common sense flew by the wayside. He ran the knuckles of his good hand along the softness of her cheek.

Had she pulled away, that would have been the end of it. But she didn't. She merely watched him, her lips parting, tempting him to take things a step further.

Ah, man. What an idiot. Why'd he have to go and do that? Stir things up. Make things complicated.

He withdrew his hand, then clicked his tongue. "I'm really sorry about that, Caitlin. I have no idea what got into me. I must have jarred my brains on the pavement."

"No, I kind of lost it, too." She fingered the place on her cheek where his knuckles had stroked. When their gazes met, she quickly looked away, and her hand dropped into her lap.

Yeah, she'd definitely lost it, too.

He got to his feet and dragged a hand though his hair. He wasn't used to women wanting to take the blame for something he should have been able to avoid, like an accident or an inappropriate caress. So he changed the subject. "Thanks for dinner, Caitlin."

"You're welcome." She followed him to the door to see him out. But something continued to hover between them. Something sensual. Something he ought to avoid, if he hadn't complicated things by making a promise to her daughter.

"I was serious about letting Emily visit Fred," he said. "Your call, of course."

"She's really attached to him."

"Okay." he said, even though he was now feeling as skittish as the psycho cat hiding under the bed. "Maybe tomorrow morning."

"That's fine." She smiled. "Then I can take you to get that rental car."

He nodded, then returned to the dark house alone. If he hadn't already told Emily she could visit, he'd board up the windows of his place and lock himself inside.

Away from the woman and kid who promised to be nothing but trouble.

Chapter Three

As Caitlin dried the last of the morning dishes, Emily waited in the breakfast nook, feet dangling from her seat, elbows resting on the table, hands propping up her chin.

"It's nine-oh-one," the little girl announced.

Each day, at roughly nine o'clock, Emily and Caitlin took the neighbor's dog for a walk. It had become a tradition they both looked forward to, a special time when she and her daughter could chat, get a little exercise and enjoy the fresh air and sunshine.

And it gave Emily another chance to pretend she had a pet of her own.

"You're sure good at telling time, Em. But just give me a minute more. I'm nearly finished." Caitlin placed the last spoon into the drawer, then folded the damp towel and hung it on the rack to dry.

"Yea!" Emily climbed from her chair, just as the telephone rang, then paused. "Oh, no."

"Sorry, sweetie. I'll make this quick." Caitlin snatched the receiver from the hook. "Hello?"

It was Phyllis McAree, her attorney. "Have you got a minute?"

Caitlin glanced at her eager daughter, then lifted her index finger, indicating the call would take a moment.

"Yes, Phyllis. Go ahead." Caitlin gripped the receiver and held her breath, hoping the competent family law specialist had something positive to report.

"From what I can gather, Zack's parole hearing has been set up for the end of the month. And since he hasn't had any problems while serving his term, there's a good chance he'll be released. I spoke to his attorney, and there's no way they'll drop the custody suit. Zack wants his child."

Caitlin's heart dropped to her stomach. Tears stung her eyes, and a lump formed in her throat, making it difficult to speak—even if Emily hadn't been in the room, listening intently.

She glanced at her daughter, the little girl who'd become the love of her life.

"It's nine-oh-three," Emily whispered.

Under other circumstances, Caitlin would have handled Emily differently. She would have told her to be patient and wait until after the phone call. But Caitlin didn't want to worry about the words she might say, the tears she might cry.

"Just a minute," she told Phyllis. Then she placed a hand over the mouthpiece of the receiver. "Em, why don't you knock on the Blackstone's door and ask if you can bring Scruffy over here."

"To our house?" Her daughter's eyes brightened. "Okay!"

Allowing Scruffy to visit hadn't been an option before, due to Caitlin's allergies. But right now, she needed some time alone. And although she didn't usually let Emily go outside unsupervised, the Blackstones shared a wall with Caitlin, and the door was merely steps away from her own. "Leave our front door open so I can watch you, honey."

"Okay." Emily grinned, then dashed outside.

"I'm sorry for the interruption," Caitlin told her attorney, "but I didn't want to talk in front of my daughter."

"I can certainly understand that." Phyllis blew out a sigh. "I won't lie to you, Caitlin. This case isn't going to be easy. Emotions will run high, and so will the legal fees. Apparently Zack has an uncle who's willing to put up the money for his fight."

Caitlin's heart sank. She hadn't counted on Zack having anyone's support. She'd heard he was an orphan, and she'd hoped a lack of finances would prohibit him from hiring an attorney.

"What are the chances that Zack will win custody?" she asked the attorney. "After all, he *is* her biological father."

"I wish I could tell you. Custody cases are never

easy to predict, but you're the only mother Emily has ever known, and that's a strong point in your favor."

But was it enough?

"Zack will probably claim to be rehabilitated," Phyllis added. "And his attorney claims he has a job lined up at the construction company, where his uncle works."

"He's still a convicted felon," Caitlin said. "Surely the courts won't put a child in his home without being sure he's really changed."

"Even if he's made a complete turnaround and plans to be a law-abiding citizen and a good father to his child, there are other factors the court will have to consider. Because he's on parole, his home will be open to random searches and seizures at any time of the day or night. It won't be a good environment for a child. And that's another argument I'll make."

A chill crept over Caitlin, and her hands shook. "What happens if Emily's at the house and they find something like drugs, weapons, some of those delinquents he used to hang around, or other parolees he met while incarcerated?"

"Zack will be sent back to prison, and social workers will take Emily to the county receiving home."

"Oh, God. I can't let that happen."

"Caitlin, I'll do everything in my power to help you. But keep in mind that you'll retain custody during the legal proceedings. Then, even if the court does decide to let Zack have Emily, the transfer would probably start with visitation."

"I don't even want her to meet him, let alone spend

unsupervised time with him." Caitlin's stomach tossed and turned, threatening to upchuck her breakfast and the coffee she'd drank.

"Let's not worry until we have something to worry about, all right?"

That was easy for the attorney to say.

Caitlin glanced out the door, spotting Emily as she stood on Gerald and Mary's porch—unaware of the father who threatened her future.

Emily smiled as the morning sunshine warmed her face. She liked being outside. But even more than that, she liked being a big girl and no longer a baby.

A bird called from the big tree on the grass. And an engine roared to a start from the carport.

It was fun to be outdoors alone. To be 'sponsible enough to go get Scruffy all by herself.

She knocked again at the Blackstone's door, this time really hard because Mary and Gerald didn't hear very good.

A minute later Gerald answered. "Why hello, Emily." He looked all around. "Where's your mommy?"

"She's talking on the phone. But she said I could come and get Scruffy all by myself and take him to my house to play. And when she's all done talking, we can go on our walk."

"You're sure getting to be a big girl," Harvey said.

Emily was glad to know he thought so, too.

Scruffy barked, as he came running, wagging his bushy tail like he was really happy to see her. That's why Emily loved the little dog. 'Cause he always kissed her face until it was all wet.

She giggled, then plopped down to her knees and let Scruffy welcome her with wags and licks and little whines.

"How about a treat?" Mary asked her. "I just baked a fresh batch of oatmeal cookies with raisins."

"No, thank you. My tummy is all filled up with breakfast." Emily pooched out her stomach and rubbed it. "See?"

"Maybe after your walk."

Emily nodded.

"Hold on a minute, Scruffy." Mr. Blackstone stooped, as he snapped the hook onto the squirmy little dog's collar, then handed Emily the leash. "Have a good time on your walk, sweetheart."

"I will." Emily gave Scruffy a big hug. "Okay, let's go get Mommy."

As Gerald closed his door, and Emily took Scruffy down the steps, the doggie pulled her onto the grass, so he could go potty. When he was all done, he started to run for the sidewalk, where Mommy and Emily usually walked. But Emily pulled him back. "Not yet, Scruffy. We gotta wait for Mommy."

Scruffy was sad, but he obeyed Emily. And that made her happy. As they walked toward Emily's house, Scruffy spotted a butterfly on the flower bush by the front door. He barked and wagged his tail.

Emily had to use both hands to hold him back. "Silly, you can't play with butterflies. God made them for us to look at. Isn't this one pretty?"

She studied the yellow and black wings. It was one of the prettiest she'd ever seen that wasn't in a picture book.

When they went on walks, Mommy let Emily and Scruffy look at things like rolly-pollies, the little gray bugs that rolled into balls when they were shy or scared.

Maybe it was okay to stay in the front yard. Mommy couldn't get mad at that. Besides, Emily wouldn't go anywhere 'cept stay on the lawn.

The butterfly flew away, toward Greg's house, where Brett was staying.

He was a nice man, just like Greg. And he'd said she could come over and visit Fred.

She got a good idea that made her smile. Maybe Brett and Fred wanted to take a walk with them.

Emily didn't know if Fred had a leash, like Scruffy did, but Brett could carry him.

"Come on, Scruffy. Let's go see our neighbors."

Brett rolled over in bed, taking the pillow and placing it over his head, blocking out the sunlight that pierced through a bent slat in the blinds.

There weren't too many mornings when he had the luxury of sleep. Besides, he'd stayed awake last night, long after he'd left Caitlin's house.

He wasn't exactly sure why he couldn't sleep. Thoughts of his son, he supposed. And the little moppet next door. Crayon drawings on refrigerators. Pretty moms he shouldn't allow to get too close.

And when he'd finally hit the sheets, he'd

dreamed of tropical breezes, setting suns and an attractive blonde who made a guy want to take a romantic, moonlit swim in the South Pacific.

The doorbell sounded, and he had half a notion to ignore it—until it rang over and over.

He cursed under his breath and climbed from bed. As a second thought, he slipped on a pair of sweatpants. Brett always slept in the raw, and there was no need to flash Greg's neighbors. Or a salesman.

Damn, he wanted to clobber whoever was leaning on the bell.

He flung open the door with a little more force than necessary, ready to snap at whoever had rudely awakened him. But when he found Emily and a little brown mutt standing on the porch, he slowly shook his head. A grin tugged at his lips.

So much for wanting to clobber whoever had been his wake-up call.

Little Emily, with her eyes glimmering, the sunlight glistening in her hair, held the dog's leash with both hands and flashed him a bubbly smile. "Hi, Brett."

"Hello there," he told the little cutie dressed in yellow and orange overalls. He scanned the yard, but didn't see anyone. "Where's your mom?"

"She's on the phone," the child said. "We're going for a walk. Do you want to go with us?"

From behind him, the psycho cat hissed.

Emily brightened, transferred the leash to her left hand, then lifted the fingers of her right in a wiggly little wave. "Hi, Fred! This is Scruffy. Want to play?"

The dog barked, and the cat wailed like its tail was on fire.

Before Brett could think, speak or react, the bushy, brown dog lurched forward, jerked the leash out of Emily's hand and tore through the house, chasing Fred.

Brett nearly cheered the dog on, hoping the cranky cat got its comeuppance. But Greg loved the damn critter. And so did Emily.

As the cat leaped over the sofa, the dog tried to follow, jumping onto the cushions, then balking at the distance. It hopped over the armrest instead.

The cat continued to wail like a banshee, and the dog barked like the devil was on its tail.

"No," Emily shrieked. "Don't do that!"

Then she dashed inside the house, hot on the trail of the dog and cat.

No! Don't do that!

Inside the kitchen, Caitlin heard her daughter's frantic scream. "Oh, my God." She dropped the telephone receiver on the floor and rushed out the front door. "Emily!"

"Over here," Brett yelled from the doorway of Greg's house. "The damn dog and cat are tearing the place apart."

Inside Greg's condo, Fred flew over chair and table, knocking over a lamp, before heading down the hall. The dog skidded on the hardwood floor, like the head of a demon-possessed dust mop.

"Stop, Scruffy!" Emily chased after the dog. "Fred is a'scared of you."

Caitlin stood on the stoop, her pulse racing, heart pounding, knees wobbling, while she waited for her brain to slow the rush of adrenaline.

Thank God her daughter wasn't being abducted. She blew out a sigh, as she joined the melee, hoping to catch the dog before the animals tore Greg's house apart.

Emily ran after Scruffy, as Scruffy ran after Fred. Rather than get caught up in a comedy of errors, Caitlin paused near the sofa and watched.

Brett, who wore only a pair of sweatpants, used strategy in waylaying the flying pooch. And she couldn't help but smile, couldn't help but watch the muscles in his back and shoulders flex, couldn't help admiring his male form.

He was a good-looking man; the kind of man most unmarried women would pursue. But she wasn't most women—she was a single mom who didn't want to jeopardize a custody battle by having a relationship at this point in time.

Moments later, Brett managed to snatch the leash and pull the dog to a halt. But he couldn't stop Fred from dashing out the front door in a flash of black fur.

Emily hunkered down on the floor and shook her finger at Scruffy. "That was a naughty thing for you to do. You need to say sorry to Fred."

Brett caught Caitlin's gaze, and something passed between them. A parenting sort of thing. Understanding that the house cat might not be safe outdoors and wanting to spare Emily any worry.

"Even if dogs could talk to cats, that would be tough," Brett told Emily. "Fred ran off."

Emily gasped. "He went outside all by himself?"

"I'm afraid so." Brett raked a hand through his hair, then glanced at Caitlin. "I'd better go look for him."

"Emily and I will help. Just let me take Scruffy back to his house."

He glanced down at his bare feet. "I'd better get on a pair of shoes and a shirt."

She nodded, then took Emily by the hand and walked the dog to Mary and Gerald's, her steps as fast as Emily's little legs could match.

A canyon bordered the complex, where coyotes sometimes howled in the evening. And recently several small pets had disappeared.

If they didn't find the runaway cat by nightfall, Fred was in big trouble.

Two hours later, after a thorough search of the neighborhood, Fred was still missing in action.

Brett had hoped they'd find the pesky cat high in a tree. At least he'd be able to get it down. And if he couldn't? He'd call the Bayside Fire Department for assistance. Firemen still did that sort of thing as a community service, didn't they?

But no such luck. The damn cat had disappeared like a ghost in the night.

As they trudged back to the front yard, Emily was in tears. "What if Fred is lost forever?"

Brett shot a glance at Caitlin and saw the anguish in her eyes. He suspected she grieved more for her hurting child than for the cat. And, he had to admit, Emily's tears were doing a real number on him, too. Poor kid.

He dropped to one knee, took Emily's hands in his and gazed into her tear-filled eyes. "Listen, honey. I've got a great idea that's sure to help us find Fred in no time at all."

She sniffled, clearly not convinced of anything but Fred's loss and possible demise. "What is it?"

"We can make some big posters to tell people in the neighborhood that Fred is missing. I'll offer a hundred dollars as a reward. And we'll give our phone numbers, so they can call us and tell us where he is."

Emily nodded, then wiped at her tears.

Brett glanced at Caitlin. "Is a hundred dollars enough? Or should I offer more?"

"I think that's plenty." She shot him a smile that tugged at his heart, making him feel like some kind of teammate. "Thanks for understanding, Brett."

He shrugged. "Greg's a good friend, and he loves the cat. Besides, I promised to look after it…" He glanced at the little blond pixie in pigtails. "And I'd do just about anything to see her smile again."

Caitlin placed a gentle hand on his shoulder, and he had the strangest urge to slip an arm around her, to accept whatever that touch meant, whatever it offered.

But he knew better than that. "Come on, let's get those posters made."

Twenty minutes later, they sat in Caitlin's house, paper and colored markers spread over the dining room table.

"Here's another picture of him." Emily passed her mother a drawing of a black cat wearing a Cheshire smile. "Do you think someone will bring Fred home if we give them big money as a prize?"

"I sure hope so, Em." Caitlin looked up at Brett, and blessed him with a smile that made him glad he'd joined her team—at least temporarily.

He cleared his throat, hoping to shed the sappy thoughts that rose whenever she looked at him like that. "What do you say we hang these posters up?"

Caitlin nibbled on her bottom lip, then asked Emily to wash her hands first. When the child left them alone, she whispered quietly. "In case the cat was hit by a car or something, maybe I'd better ask Mary and Gerald Blackstone to watch Emily for me."

Hell, he hadn't thought about that. Fred had been a house cat all of his life and didn't have any street smarts. "You're right. Emily doesn't need to see anything like that."

When the little girl returned, Caitlin picked up the posters. "Emily, you can help us put up the first one on the streetlight by our house. But Brett and I are going to place the others throughout the neighborhood."

"Okay." She looked up at him. "I hope someone calls us right away."

So did Brett.

He knew that having a pet die was part of life. But Emily was too young, too innocent to learn that Fred had become roadkill.

And he wasn't looking forward to telling Greg

that Fred had lost all nine of his lives while Brett was on duty.

Minutes later, after the first poster had been attached to the lamppost and Emily had been delivered to the Blackstones, Caitlin and Brett took off on their trek to advertise a reward for Fred's safe return.

The sun warmed their backs, as they strode through the neighborhood.

"I can't imagine where he went," she said.

"Neither can I. But the reward ought to make someone step forward."

"I hope so."

Her shoulder brushed his arm, and he had the weirdest urge to take her hand. But a move like that would only get him in trouble.

He didn't date women with kids. And this *thing* with Caitlin and Emily—whatever it was—had grown too cozy for comfort. But he couldn't quit now. Not until he found Fred.

Or a convincing replacement.

Hey, that wasn't a bad idea. All he had to do was find a big, fluffy black cat. Maybe no one would notice. He sure as hell couldn't see anything about Fred that a million other black cats didn't have. Except for that psycho personality.

They posted signs near the playground, the laundry room, the community mailboxes and the rec room. And when they'd finally placed them all, they headed home.

"That ought to do it." Brett glanced at Caitlin and saw her lip tremble. Oh, for cripes sake. She wasn't going to cry, was she? About the cat?

She looked up in a moment of weakness, but didn't speak.

"Are you sad for Fred or for Emily?"

"Emily," she said, voice whisper soft.

"I'll find that cat. One way or another. Don't worry."

She flashed him a watery-eyed smile. "It's not just the cat."

"What is it?"

She slowly shook her head. "Nothing."

He didn't believe her. But for some reason, his arm lifted, slipped around her and drew her close. "It'll be okay. I promise."

"Thanks," she said. But the look in her eyes told him she didn't believe him.

As her petite body, soft and perfect, molded to his side, as her tropical scent taunted him, tempted him, he slowly dropped his arm. Letting go. Backing off.

He was getting entirely too close to his pretty neighbor. And as soon as that damn cat returned— or its replacement was found—Brett was going to keep his door locked, his blinds pulled.

And his libido in check.

Caitlin and her daughter spelled trouble—with a crooked *T* and a backwards *R*.

Chapter Four

Two days later, on a Saturday afternoon, Fred still hadn't returned. And no one had responded to the posters placed all over the complex.

Where the hell could that crazy animal be?

Brett didn't think Fred would get close enough to a stranger to get catnapped.

Did dogcatchers pick up cats?

He wasn't sure, but he called the Bayside Animal Shelter, just in case.

A man answered, and Brett asked if they'd found a black stray cat.

"We have forty-six adults and nine kittens, many of which are strays," the guy told him. "You'll have to come look for yourself."

He thought about driving over by himself, then had second thoughts. If Fred couldn't stand the sight of Brett in the house, how would he react in a moving vehicle?

Maybe it would be easier if he had Caitlin and Emily with him.

When he knocked on the door of Caitlin's condo, Emily answered. Her eyes shimmered with hope. "Did someone call and tell you they have Fred?"

"Not yet," he admitted. "But I thought it might be a good idea if we went to the dog pound and looked for him."

"Fred hates dogs," the child said. "Why would he go there?"

Caitlin joined them at the door, wearing a pale green sundress and a warm smile. "Brett is talking about the animal shelter, honey. They take care of lost dogs and cats until the owners can be found."

Or until a pet was mistakenly "put to sleep" before a kid arrived to take him home.

When Brett was a boy, his dog Scooter dug under the fence and ran off. But by the time his dad had gotten around to checking with the pound, Scooter had been killed.

A snafu of some kind, the animal control officer had explained. But that hadn't made a grieving kid feel any better.

Brett caught the pretty mother's gaze. "I called this morning, and they've got a lot of strays. I think we'd better go look as soon as possible." He didn't explain why they shouldn't drag their feet.

"All right. I'll get my purse."

Fifteen minutes later, Brett pulled the Ford Expedition he'd rented into the parking lot of the Bayside Animal Shelter.

"Do you mind if I wait here?" Caitlin asked. "My allergies will probably kick up if I go inside."

"Sure." Brett helped Emily from the back seat. "Come on. Let's go see if we can find Fred."

They bypassed the office and set out on their own search, finding cage after cage filled with dogs—big ones, little ones, old ones, young ones. Black. Brown. Some quiet, some barking and one tricolored mutt howling like a wolf with its paw in a trap.

Brett thought of Scooter, a kid's best friend who'd spent his last days locked in a place like this. Even now, as an adult, he remembered a child's pain at the loss of a pet.

Up ahead, he spotted a gray block structure. A sign on a door said Cattery.

"Come on, Emily." He took the child's hand. "Let's look in here. I think this is where they keep the cats."

And he was right.

Inside they found felines of all colors and sizes. Long hair, short hair. He scanned the place looking for Fred—or a look-alike that could serve as a replacement.

In cage number 46, a big black cat was curled up on a red towel. Even Brett, who didn't particularly like animals other than dogs, knew it wasn't Fred. But he pointed anyway. "Look, Emily. There he is."

She eased toward the cage and peered through the bars. "That's not him."

"How do you know?"

"Fred has yellow eyes. And a little white dot on his chin."

Brett, obviously, hadn't noticed the psycho cat's uniqueness.

Well, he'd tried. Tricking Emily with another cat wasn't going to work.

"Oh, look." She pointed her finger to a cage near the floor, where two kittens sniffed at the bars on the door. "See the gray one and the little orange one? Aren't they cute?"

He didn't know about that; he'd always been a dog person. But he noticed how the two kittens had piqued her interest and made her temporarily forget her loss.

She squatted on the floor, her face eye level with the cage door, and reached her fingers through the bars.

Brett continued to peruse the room, searching for Fred. But the darn critter was still M.I.A.

Emily giggled. "They're so cute and funny."

As he watched the child, an idea formed. Would a new kitten help her forget about the cat that ran away?

A dark-haired, middle-aged woman entered the cattery, wearing a Captain Kangaroo-style apron and a badge that announced she was a volunteer. "Let me know if you'd like me to take any of these kitties out of the cage so you can play with them."

Emily's eyes brightened, as she pointed to the two kittens wrestling in their cage. "Can we play with these?"

"Of course." The woman opened the door and took

both kittens from the pen and set them on the floor. "The orange tabby is a little girl, the gray is a boy."

Brett watched as Emily laughed at the kittens' antics, then cuddled each one. Her mood had certainly lifted.

And both the tabby and the gray had pleasant personalities, a lot nicer than that ornery cat she was missing.

Maybe he ought to adopt one of those as a replacement for Fred. Of course, he wasn't sure how Greg would feel about having a different cat, but Brett would face his friend later, after Greg had returned from his vacation. Right now, his primary goal was getting Emily over her sadness.

Ah, what the hell.

"Which one should we get, Emily?"

Her eyes widened. "We get to take one home?"

"Sure."

A smile flashed on her face, but she quickly reeled it in. "Mommy is 'lergic."

Brett knew that. And he certainly didn't want a kitten underfoot. But he didn't want to see Emily all torn up over Fred, either. "Choose the one you think Greg will like best, since we'll have to take it to his house to live."

She glanced at the little balls of fluff, then looked at Brett with peepers that turned his backbone to mush. "But if I pick Princess, Fluffy will feel bad."

She'd named them already?

"Greg wouldn't want us to leave Fluffy behind to get lonely," she added.

Or to be put to sleep.

Brett wasn't sure how his buddy would feel about a new kitten, let alone two. But right now, the important thing was making the child happy.

And putting some distance between himself and her pretty mother. At least they wouldn't be bumping elbows while they made posters and brushing arms as they walked through the neighborhood looking for a runaway cat that was probably part of the canyon ecosystem by now.

"Okay," he told the volunteer. "We'll take them both."

The woman grinned. "Good choice, sir. I'll show you to the front desk so you can pay for them."

Emily handed Brett the orange tabby. "This one is Princess."

He really didn't like cats, but he took the little thing in his arms. It was kind of cute. And a hell of a lot sweeter than crotchety old Fred.

"This one is Fluffy," Emily told him, as she cuddled the shorthaired gray male.

"Come along with me," the volunteer said, as she led them back to the office.

A man dressed in a blue shirt with a Bayside Animal Shelter logo handed Brett paperwork to complete. And there was a ton of it, too.

They wanted to know the size of the home and yard, whether the animal would live outdoors or in. There were even questions about how people ought to discipline pets.

He'd taken psychological evals in the Navy, but

he never expected to get the third-degree at a dog pound. He supposed they were just trying to make sure the animals would find good owners.

Do you own your home or rent?

Brett didn't do either. Greg had offered to let him buy into his place, but he hadn't wanted to be tied down.

"Why do you want to know whether I own a home or not?" he asked the clerk.

"If you rent, we'll need an authorization from the landlord before allowing the adoption."

Oh, for cripes sake. He glanced at Emily, saw the light in her eyes.

He placed an *X* next to Own. Hey, that really wasn't a lie. Not if Brett was adopting a pet for Greg by proxy.

After the slightly balding desk clerk went over Brett's answers, he uttered a few "uh-huhs" and "hmmms" before approving the adoption.

Brett hadn't mentioned his deployments or the fact that he wouldn't be able to care for a pet 24/7. He knew better than to offer that information. But he intended to give the cats to Greg. And if his buddy didn't want them? Then he'd figure out a way to convince him he did. Bribery being the first idea that came to mind.

"That will be two hundred and twenty dollars," the man behind the desk said.

Brett just about dropped the orange tabby he held in his left arm. "How much?"

"Two hundred and twenty dollars."

"For two stray kittens? You gotta be shittin…" He

glanced at Emily, at the bright-eyed smile on her face. "You've got to be kidding. What are they, *purebreds?*"

"Well, the charge to adopt is seventy-five dollars apiece. That includes a medical exam, a flea dip and worming. Then there's a thirty-five dollar spaying deposit. When you show proof that you've had the kittens neutered, we'll return the money."

Brett grimaced as he reached for his wallet and peeled out the bills.

The clerk accepted his payment, then gave him a ten-dollar-off coupon for the Bayside Pet Supply Center and a list of area vets that would spay the kittens.

Brett didn't jump into anything without giving it a good deal of thought and planning. So he wasn't exactly sure how he'd gotten caught up in this whole pet-owner thing. And he had a sneaking suspicion he'd taken on more than he could handle.

Or more than he wanted to handle.

What the hell would he do if Greg didn't want two kittens?

But when he looked at the happy child, he shrugged. "Okay, let's take Fluffy and Princess home."

"Just a moment," the clerk said. "You'll need a carrier to take them in the car."

"What?"

"It's our policy. We can't let them go home without a carrier."

"I don't have one."

"Well, we have special transport boxes for ten dollars each." He lifted a carton with holes in it.

"It's just a cardboard box," Brett said.

"It's a recyclable carrier we offer as a service to new pet owners." The man behind the counter handed one to Brett. "Safety first."

Feeling like a sucker who'd just rubbed elbows with P.T. Barnum, Brett forked over another ten bucks. "Come on, Emily. Let's get out of here before they tax us for loitering."

As he carried the box of kittens out of the office, Emily slipped her hand in his, making him feel as though he'd done the right thing—rather than something stupid.

Then she gave his hand a little squeeze, as though they were a team.

A team Brett knew better than to join.

Caitlin opened the passenger door of the Explorer, hoping to catch a better breeze. It had grown hot waiting in the parking lot.

She glanced at her wristwatch. What was keeping them? Had they found Fred?

Tired of waiting and wondering what was going on, she climbed from the SUV to join Brett and Emily, in spite of her allergies. But before she could take two steps, she spotted her handsome neighbor and her daughter walking out the office door. Brett carried a cardboard box with air holes in his left hand.

Oh, thank goodness. They'd found Fred.

Emily, who was grinning from ear to ear, was practically skipping along the sidewalk. "Guess what, Mommy. Brett bought two new kitties, Fluffy and Princess."

She glanced at the rugged Navy helicopter pilot who wore an interesting expression—one she'd describe as a sheepish scowl. He helped Emily into the back seat, set the box next to her, then slid behind the wheel.

When he caught Caitlin's gaze, she said, "I thought you were just going to look for Fred."

He shrugged. "Emily fell in love with these little guys. And heck, it's good to see her smiling again, don't you think?"

"Yes, I suppose so. But you'll have to keep them at Greg's." She buckled her seat belt, hoping her allergies didn't kick up on the ride home.

As Emily talked through the little holes to the new kittens, Caitlin snuck a glance at Brett. He obviously wasn't a cat lover. And he'd agreed to adopt two kittens, just to make her daughter happy. "Thank you. That was awfully sweet of you."

He caught her gaze, that sheepish expression touching her heart. "I had to do something."

"But what if…" She glanced in the rearview mirror, then back at him, then spelled out, "F-R-E-D C-O-M-E-S B-A-C-K?"

"I…uh, hadn't thought about that." He looked over his shoulder at Emily and the box that contained the kittens. "I'll have to deal with that when the time comes, I guess."

Before she could respond, she sneezed.

"Bless you."

"Thanks."

Ten minutes and three sneezes later, they pulled into the complex, where several of the neighbors had already begun setting plastic chairs and portable tables on the lawn near the rec room. Gerald and another man fiddled with Tiki lights.

"What's going on?" Brett asked.

"We're having a community luau. It's a lot of fun. And the food is incredible, since it's a potluck." She flashed him a smile. "You're going, aren't you?"

He scrunched his face. "To a potluck? I don't know. I'll have to think about it."

She didn't know exactly why she wanted to encourage his attendance, but she did. "It'll give you a chance to meet other people who live in the complex."

He didn't respond, and she suspected he wasn't one who regularly socialized with neighbors.

"What's holding you back?" she asked.

He shrugged. "I haven't lived in a neighborhood for years. And those community functions never interested me."

"Oh, come on. What are you going to do? Stay home and watch us eat, drink and be merry from the window?"

"I guess I could go buy something ready-made."

"I'm making a potato salad for Emily and I. Why don't I make something for you to take?"

"I hate to ask you to do that."

"It's no trouble." And it wasn't. She loved to cook. And she'd wanted to try out Mary's Texas Chocolate Cake recipe.

She sneezed again, and her eyes watered.

"Bless you twice. It looks like the cats are playing havoc with your allergies."

"You're right. Even though they're in a box, we're in close quarters."

"I'll get the cats out of here." Brett climbed from the SUV, then opened Emily's door, took the box and helped the child out of her car seat.

"Can I go with you?" Emily asked Brett. "I want to show Princess and Fluffy where the water and food and litter box is."

"Do you mind?" Brett caught Caitlin's gaze. "I'll bring her home in a few minutes."

"All right." She watched Brett carry the box of kittens and lead her daughter to Greg's condo. The man was proving to be every bit as good a neighbor and friend as Greg had been. Maybe more so.

Trouble was, she hadn't been the least bit attracted to Greg.

After getting Fluffy and Princess settled and allowing Emily to play with the kitties she considered her pets, Brett walked the little girl home. As they entered Caitlin's condo, which seemed homier than ever, the aroma of something sweet baking in the oven snagged Brett's attention, as well as tweaked his appetite. Something chocolate maybe?

"Mommy," Emily called out, "we're home."

"I'm in the kitchen," her mother replied.

They found Caitlin standing at the counter, wearing the same pale green sundress that set off the color of her eyes, making them a deep-sea green. She'd pulled her hair up in a twist, using a brass clip to hold the golden strands. And she'd slipped off her shoes.

She looked comfortable, at home in the kitchen. A nester, who was too damn appealing, and *so* not his type.

She looked up from a pile of chopped pickles and favored them both with a smile. "How did the kitties like their new home?"

"They like Fred's climby thing and his toys," Emily said. "And I'm sure he won't mind sharing with them."

Caitlin glanced at Brett, and he knew they were both questioning whether Fred would return.

"He's going to be so surprised when he comes home. And Princess and Fluffy will be happy, too. They were so sad when I had to leave."

Her mother smiled. "Maybe you can see them later today, after your nap."

"Then I better hurry up and go to sleep so I can wake up," Emily said. Then she looked at Brett. "Will you still be here?"

"Probably not, but you can come by later to see the cats." He glanced at Caitlin. "That is, if your mother says it's okay."

So much for hoping to put some distance between him and his neighbors.

Caitlin brushed a kiss on Emily's head. "We'll see. Why don't you wash your hands, then go lay down."

As Emily left the room, Brett figured it was time for him to cut out. But for some reason, his feet wouldn't move. The coziness of Caitlin's home, the tantalizing aroma from the oven held him steady. And he hoped to hell that was all that had a hold on him.

"Something sure smells good," he said.

"It's a chocolate cake. And that reminds me…" She

turned on the oven light, then peered into the window on the door. The pale green fabric of her dress caressed the gentle curve of her hips. And the hem lifted in back, giving him a glimpse of shapely legs. "It's nearly done."

As she turned to face him, he glanced at the countertop, so she wouldn't know he'd been looking at her, admiring her curves, her figure. Letting his thoughts go in a direction they shouldn't.

"The cake is your contribution to the luau." Her smile lit up the warm kitchen, making his heart constrict in a goofy way.

"Thanks." He studied her for a moment, the way a strand of hair brushed her cheek, the way she made chopping pickles look interesting. Enticing.

He ought to excuse himself, but for some reason, he wasn't ready to go home to an empty house. "What's with the community luau?"

"It's an annual event put on by the homeowners association. They roast a pig in the ground and provide Hawaiian music from speakers in the clubhouse. And the residents all chip in with salads and desserts." She returned to chopping pickles, then took a fork and checked the potatoes boiling in a large pot on the stove. "I hope these are going to be okay. I started them before we went to the animal shelter and turned them off before they were done."

When she picked up two potholders and tried to lift the pot, he stopped her. "Let me do that."

She stepped out of the way, and he poured off the water for her. A blast of steam rose from the sink.

"Now what?" he asked.

"I'll put them in the colander until they cool off a bit." She reached into the cupboard and pulled out a blue plastic strainer, then took a pair of tongs from the drawer.

"I'll do that." He wasn't exactly sure where his words came from.

She studied him for a moment, as though his efforts to be helpful had surprised her, then handed him the metal tongs.

As he reached for the utensil, their fingers touched, lingered. A shiver of heat shimmied up his arm, stimulating his pulse.

But he shook it off the best he could and placed the steaming hot potatoes into the strainer. When he'd finished, he turned and faced her. "Now what?"

She crossed her arms and lifted a brow. "You want to help me cook?"

Well, not that he was consciously aware of. But something about being here—with her—felt right. And he'd be damned if he knew why.

So he wagered a guess. "I don't really know my way around the kitchen, but if you gave me an easy job, something Emily might be able to do, it would make me feel more like a real contributor to the potluck."

"Then by all means, feel free to wash the celery and cut it into pieces." Her playful smile struck a goofy chord in his chest, making him feel a little too domestic for comfort.

But heck. He didn't have anything to do at home. And if he went to the potluck, he would eat his fill. So he might as well help her make the salad.

After chopping the celery, they worked on the potatoes together. And then he watched as she mixed the ingredients in a large bowl.

She added salt and pepper, then dug in a spoon and offered him a taste.

He allowed her to feed him, which was kind of weird and nice at the same time.

"What do you think?" she asked.

"It's good."

"We'll let it sit for awhile so the flavors can blend." Then she reached for the plastic wrap, covered the bowl and placed it in the refrigerator.

He wasn't sure why it fascinated him to watch her move about the kitchen. It's not like he found cooking to be anything special. He was a take-out guy. Fast food. Anything that allowed him to stay away from an empty house.

When the timer went off, she removed a chocolate sheet cake from the oven.

Ooh boy, did it smell good.

"While the cake cools a bit, I'll show you how to make fudge frosting." She flashed him a grin that would tempt even a man without a sweet tooth. Then she proceeded to cook a chocolate frosting on the stove, adding chopped nuts. And when she'd finished, she offered him a taste.

But it wasn't the chocolate on the spoon he wanted to taste. It was the cook holding him prisoner in her kitchen.

As she lifted the frosting to his lips, he took hold of her hand, guiding the spoon into his mouth. But their gazes locked, their movements slowed. Sexual awareness settled around him. And around her, too, he suspected.

As he opened his mouth to take a bite, her lips parted, too—as though she was feeding herself at the same time.

An overwhelming urge to kiss her settled over him, and he almost succumbed to temptation. But he didn't.

Wow. It was hot in here. And not from the heat of the oven.

"How does it taste?" she asked, her voice softer than it had been before.

It tasted too damned good—like something that wasn't healthy if one overindulged. "Delicious," he told her, before stepping back, away from temptation. "Well, I'd better go. I'll, uh, see you at the luau."

"All right."

As he turned to leave, his hunger raged for a woman he suspected was much sweeter than sugar and chocolate. But he wouldn't falter, wouldn't indulge, wouldn't taste.

Because if he kissed her, he wasn't sure what would happen next. And that was enough to completely scare the hell out of a guy who'd once been a hellion.

A guy who valued his rebellious streak and his desire to fly solo.

Chapter Five

As the sun dropped over the bay, the residents of the Ocean Breeze condominium complex began to gather on the lawn.

They either stood in small, intimate groups or sat at the tables and chairs the luau committee had set up.

Brett kept a polite distance. He'd always felt like an outsider at neighborhood get-togethers like this. Still, he listened to the pleasantries and shared laughter and made small talk whenever necessary.

When he'd been married to Kelly, she'd always gotten excited about summer block parties, those social gatherings the neighbors used to hold in the cul-de-sac of Periwinkle Lane.

Did they still drag out lawn chairs and enjoy a

glass of iced tea or diet soda, while they watched their kids ride big wheel bicycles and roller-skate on the sidewalks?

Probably so.

Kelly had always been a ringleader when it came to things like that.

He glanced at a group of boys playing catch on the lawn, each wearing a variety of different baseball caps. All Little Leaguers, he suspected.

A couple of men—dads, he assumed—joined in the game, giving the kids pointers.

Brett had given up organized sports as a boy, but not because he didn't like to play on a ball team. His parents hadn't been able to keep their animosity out of the stands or keep their arguments in the courtroom. His dad's frozen glares and his mother's snide comments had always clouded the joy of sports, mocking the idea of fair play and healthy competition his coach had tried to instill in him and his teammates.

And quite frankly, his folks had embarrassed the hell out of him.

If they'd ever figured out why he'd refused to play baseball anymore, they hadn't said.

He shoved his hands in the pockets of his khaki shorts and scanned the festive lawn area. The boys weren't the only ones having fun.

Emily sat near a yellow-flowered hibiscus plant, playing dolls with two other girls, both of whom appeared to be older than her—school-age.

Justin's age.

He wasn't sure why he'd never felt comfortable

at these family-type functions before. But he certainly knew why he didn't like them now. They slammed into his memories, tore open his gut.

"I got it, I got it," a boy about Justin's age yelled as he reached to snag a pop-up. The grin he wore when he caught the ball was priceless.

A real gut-wrenching heart-warmer.

Brett grabbed a beer from one of the coolers near the roped off area where the pork roasted underground. He popped the top and took a swig.

The scent of Hawaiian-barbecued meat mingled with the ocean breeze, taunting his appetite and making him wonder when they would eat.

Soon, probably. At least he hoped so. He was ready to call it a day.

He surveyed the crowd until he spotted Caitlin, something he'd been doing all afternoon. And he'd be damned if he knew why. Maybe because she was the only one he really knew in the complex.

She laughed as she worked along with two other women, lining up bowls and platters of food on a long table. He could tell she was happy, that she was comfortable and liked her neighbors.

A couple of guys in their late twenties, who were in a group playing volleyball on the grass near the laundry room, had been eyeing her throughout the late afternoon. Every once in a while, they glanced at Emily.

Did they see the child as a hindrance to a romantic relationship?

Brett did, but not because he didn't like kids or

didn't want to raise another man's child. He wanted to steer clear of potential parenting disputes.

Of course, Caitlin said Emily's father had never been a part of his daughter's life, which left Caitlin to raise the girl on her own. But even though Emily's father was out of the picture, that didn't mean Brett was a family man. So he'd have to steer clear of a romantic entanglement with the single mother—no matter how pretty, how attractive he found her.

Apparently oblivious to the male interest she'd sparked, Caitlin left the food table and moved easily through the crowd. Again, Brett was drawn to her smile, to the lilt of her voice as she spoke or laughed.

She wore a cream-colored sweatshirt and a pair of lime green shorts—nothing fancy. Yet she was the most attractive woman here. A nurse, a good cook. A homemaker.

Without a doubt, Caitlin would make some lucky man a great wife—if the guy was inclined to think of himself as family material.

"Hey there, young fellow."

Brett turned to see a gray-haired man wearing a Hawaiian shirt and a pair of slacks approach.

"We haven't been officially introduced," the seventy-something man said, "but I'm Gerald Blackstone, retired United States Marines. I hear you're a Navy man."

Brett introduced himself, and they shook hands.

"Caitlin says you're a buddy of Greg's," Gerald said.

Brett nodded. "Yes, sir."

"And that you're a helicopter pilot and fly Sea Hawks."

"That's right."

Gerald gave a slow whistle, then he grinned broadly, and his blue eyes lit up. "I'm going to have to take you down to the V.F.W. hall with me someday. When Greg's in town, he and I go have a couple of drinks with some of the old-timers and shoot the breeze."

Brett had always enjoyed talking about aircraft and sharing military stories, especially with veterans. "Sounds like fun."

Unable to help himself, he stole another glance at Caitlin and found her at a table, where she sipped a glass of wine and talked to a dark-haired woman who held a toddler in her arms.

What was with this crazy fascination? The attachment he felt, as though this had been a date and they'd arrived together.

"Caitlin is a special lady," Gerald said.

So much for surreptitious glances. Brett had been caught with his eyes on the cookie jar. "You're right. She's a good mother and a nice neighbor."

"Yep." Gerald bent, reached into the cooler and pulled out a light beer. "She sure could use someone in her corner right now."

Brett figured the old man was trying to be a matchmaker, so he decided to sidestep the issue. "She seems to be doing okay on her own."

"On the outside, I suppose." Gerald popped the tab, then took a slow, steady swig of his beer. "Things could get pretty hairy for her in the next few weeks."

"What do you mean?"

Gerald merely studied him, as though realizing he'd spoken out of turn. "Hey, looks like they're getting ready to carve the pork."

A typical hungry man's comment? Or an attempt to change the subject?

Curiosity niggled at him, and he had the urge to press the older man for an explanation. But he held his tongue.

Brett was already in too deep with his pretty, blond neighbor.

And rather than get sucked in deeper, he needed to swim against the current and get back on shore.

In fact, after he feasted on barbecue pork and potluck, he intended to do just that.

Caitlin hadn't lied about the food. The spread was amazing—and delicious.

Brett especially enjoyed the vast array of desserts, like Mary Blackstone's strawberry-rhubarb pie, which Caitlin had forced him to try. Heck, he didn't even know what a rhubarb looked like. But after one bite, he'd scarfed down two helpings.

When he'd eaten his fill, he leaned back in his chair and thought about calling it a night.

But the feast wasn't the end of the evening's festivities. Before he could thank Caitlin for inviting him and excuse himself, a heavyset woman instructed everyone to turn their chairs and face a mock stage on the lawn.

Oh, what the heck. He supposed it wouldn't hurt to sit here a bit longer, next to Caitlin and her daughter.

Emily, who held a curly-haired doll in her arms, tapped him on the knee. "Can I sit with you, Brett?"

He glanced at her mother, although he wasn't sure why. For permission?

She smiled warmly, so he opened his arms. Emily, with her hair smelling little-girl fresh, climbed in his lap, popped a thumb in her mouth and rested her head against his chest. She was just a little bit of a thing, sweet and trusting. And holding her made him feel warm and sappy at the same time.

When a parade of homely, odd-shaped hula dancers cut across the lawn and made their way to the stage, the crowd roared in laughter.

A group of burly men, some with old military tattoos, wore grass skirts, coconut shell bikini tops tied to hairy chests and hibiscus flowers stuck on bouffant wigs. Gerald Blackstone was one of them, and Brett couldn't help but laugh at the retired marine who was really hamming it up.

Canned ukulele music played in the background, as the men gyrated their hips and fluttered their arms and fingers, putting on one heck of a show.

But Emily, who was usually vibrant and full of life, hadn't uttered a sound or moved a muscle. Didn't she think it was funny?

Brett glanced at her face and saw her eyes closed, her lips parted in exhaustion. He couldn't help but grin.

"Is she asleep?" Caitlin whispered.

He nodded, afraid to shift, to move, to wake her.

"If you don't mind holding her while I take my dishes home, I'll come back and take her to bed."

Brett adjusted the child, then slowly stood. "I'll carry her home for you."

Caitlin slid him an appreciative smile, one that said she didn't get much help in that department and made him feel like a guy who'd been given a shiny medal for doing nothing at all.

"Thank you," she said. "I'd appreciate that."

As he made his way across the lawn to Caitlin's door, waiting for her to grab her dishes and catch up, he held Emily to his chest and watched her sleep. She looked like one of those pictures of a dozing cherub—an angel with a smudge of dirt on her face, a yellow barrette dangling in her hair and a baby doll wrapped in limp arms.

A moment later, Caitlin joined him at her front porch. She carried an empty bowl that had once held her potato salad—the best he'd ever eaten—and a platter of chocolate crumbs. The cake had disappeared before Brett could go back for seconds.

Caitlin let him inside, set the dishes on a table by the door, then led him to Emily's room, where she drew back a pink-checkered comforter, revealing clean white sheets. "I don't want to wake her by putting on her pajamas yet. Just lay her down, and I'll slip off her sandals. Then, after I'm sure she's sound asleep, I'll wash her face and hands and change her clothes."

He placed the little girl on the bed, her head on the pillow, then watched as the mother brushed a kiss across her brow.

It was, he decided, an interesting and rare glimpse

of life in a sugar-and-spice world—the kind of world every child deserved, but not enough of them were blessed with.

As they left Emily's bedroom, Caitlin asked if Brett wanted a cup of coffee. "It won't take me but a minute to brew a pot."

He really ought to hightail it home, but for some reason he agreed.

Curiosity, he told himself. That's all. He just wanted to know more about Caitlin. To know why she needed someone in her corner. Why things might be hairy for her in the upcoming days.

He followed her to the kitchen and watched as she made coffee in a pot that wasn't much bigger than those provided in a motel room. As the water brewed, they made small talk and laughed about the kind of "hula girl" Gerald had made.

In no time at all, Caitlin poured two cups of coffee, sweetened hers with sugar and a dab of cream, then led Brett to the porch at the back of her house, away from the few who still partied in front.

They sat on padded seats at a glass-topped wrought iron table and listened to the night sounds of crickets chirping and the faint chords of Hawaiian music as the luau began to wind down.

A silvery moon peered out from behind a cloud. Tiki-style lights that lined the sidewalk leading to the community pool, along with Caitlin's tropical scent, reminded Brett of a romantic stretch of sidewalk along Kaanapali Beach in Maui.

It was a bit more romantic than he would have

liked, more tempting than was wise, but there was no graceful way to cut out now—even if he wanted to. So he decided to focus the conversation on something other than moonlit nights, sea breezes and romance.

"You're a good mother," he said. "And you've made a great home for Emily."

"Thank you." She took a sip of coffee. "I've tried very hard to give her the things I never had."

"Kids don't need things to make them happy." Brett could attest to that.

"I'm not talking about money or possessions." Her smile flickered, faltered, and he wasn't sure whether he should press her or not.

But he did. "What did you miss out on?"

Caitlin didn't know how much she wanted to reveal. She'd put it all behind her now and was trying her best to provide Emily with a loving, stable home—a single-parent home. "I had a sad childhood, let's just leave it at that."

Her past wasn't something she liked to share with people, especially a handsome helicopter pilot who would only be a transient in her life.

"What about you?" she asked. "Did you have a nice childhood?"

"I grew up in the lap of luxury, with every toy, game and opportunity an only child could imagine. But I doubt my childhood was any happier than yours." He took a sip of the fresh brew. "My parents loved me, but they fought constantly. And their divorce didn't end the battles. Their legal war lasted for years, and I became a pawn."

"I'm sorry." Caitlin, more than anyone, realized a child's happiness wasn't dependent upon wealth, but rather love and a home.

"Rumor had it that when my parents headed back to court, it took a forklift to carry the boxes of legal briefs and files." He laughed, but the tone held a hollow ring. "Of course, that was nothing compared to the battles that went on at home."

"Even after they separated?"

He nodded. "My mom would make promises, saying things like, 'If you tell the judge you want to live with me, I'll get you that brand-new bike you've been wanting.' And my father would counter with, 'How'd you like good ol' dad to get you that new computer with all the bells and whistles.'"

"It's too bad that they put you in the middle."

"They didn't realize the damage they were doing to me. As the years went on, the fight raged and their carrots only got bigger. So I worked them to my advantage. I got a brand-new car before I was old enough to drive and, eventually, I gained unofficial access to a hefty trust fund my grandfather had left me."

She watched him over the rim of his cup, saw the frown, the furrowed brow. "But it looks as though you survived intact."

His emotion-filled gaze locked on hers, drawing her in. "Yes, but no thanks to my parents. By the time I was a senior in high school, I'd gotten tired of the endless trips to court and their heated arguments, so I decided to make a few headlines of my own."

Somehow, she knew he wasn't talking about gaining attention for being an honor student, an Eagle Scout or an athlete. "How'd you do that?"

"I rebelled. Even when my parents finally made a half-assed attempt to bury the hatchet, my anger and resentment had festered to the point of delinquency—fighting, truancy, destruction of property, mischievous pranks, you name it. I actually enjoyed dragging my parents and my stepfather before the judge—like they'd done to me."

"I assume the Navy was your saving grace."

"Eventually. But it was Harry Logan who actually turned my life around."

"Who is Harry Logan?"

"A police detective, now retired, who has a way of reaching the heart of an angry kid. Harry took me under his wing, introduced me to a Navy pilot and things sort of took off from there."

Caitlin would've loved to have someone in her corner, someone willing to fight for her best interests. But as it was, she was forced to rely on herself.

Brett leaned back in his seat and stretched out his legs. Caitlin had a hard time not admiring him. He wore a pair of khaki slacks—expensive. And a pale green Tommy Bahama shirt that was appropriate for a luau.

When she glanced at his stunning, wild-blue-yonder eyes, she realized he was studying her, too—in a pleasing way, in a way that warmed her heart and blood. In a way that could make a single mother remember what life had been like when she was younger, carefree and without a child to consider.

He fiddled with the cup in his hands, then caught her eye. "For a kid with a sad childhood, you managed to turn out okay, too."

"I was in and out of foster homes most of my life. But when I turned thirteen, I was determined to improve my lot in life. I studied hard, graduated from high school, then applied for grants and student loans so I could attend college."

"Where you became a nurse and learned how to apply Hello Kitty bandages and mend battered motorcyclists," he supplied.

She laughed. "That's about the size of it. I got a college degree and a small place of my own." She turned, gazed through the screen of the sliding glass door, then smiled at him. "Well, actually, I rent this place, but I'd love to own it someday."

"I'm sure, with your determination, you will. I guess we both made the best of crappy childhoods." He flashed her a thought-provoking smile. One that made her wonder what hid behind it. The secrets. The pain he hadn't shared.

She could see it there, hiding deep in his eyes, and it tugged at her heart.

As much as she hated to admit it, she was drawn to Brett Tanner, to his rugged good looks, to the kindness he'd shown her and her daughter. To the way he'd turned his life around. "I'm sorry for the child you once were, but I like the man you've become."

He shrugged, as though uneasy with her praise, and she wasn't sure why. Then he slowly got to his feet. "Well, I'd better let you turn in. It's been a long day. Thanks for the coffee." He picked up the cups and saucers, slid open the screen of the sliding glass door and carried them into the house.

Caitlin followed, assuming they'd left the romantic ambiance on the patio, along with the Tiki lights, the island music and a Bella Luna moon. But in the kitchen, Brett lingered, and so did an awkward sexual awareness.

Did he feel it, too? That urge to gaze, to touch, to make the evening last a little longer?

He nodded at the cups in his hands. "Is it all right if I just set these on the counter?"

"Sure."

The intimacy they'd shared seemed to require more than a "See you later," but Caitlin wasn't sure how much more.

They stood there for a while, as though their friendship, or whatever it was, had reached a new level, an awkward level.

"Well, I'd better turn in," he said.

She nodded, then followed him to the front door.

As he reached for the knob, he paused, dropped his arm and turned. "Thanks for encouraging me to attend that luau. The food was great. And the hula dancers put on an entertaining show."

"I'm glad you enjoyed the evening."

He glanced at his feet, then raked a hand through his hair. "Listen, I'm sorry for running off at the mouth about my childhood."

So he'd been feeling guilt, not sexual attraction. That should offer her a big sense of relief, since she wasn't ready to have a man in her life, especially one who wouldn't be around forever.

So where did the disappointment come from?

"I don't usually spill my guts like that," he added.

She didn't either, but she didn't think he'd revealed too much—unless he was as discreet about his past as she was of hers. She offered him a sympathetic smile. "If anyone can understand how kids get caught up in the problems facing their parents, it's me. Don't think anything of it."

Then she gave him a hug. Nothing big, just one of those casual, almost meaningless things.

But when his arms wrapped around her, too, drawing her close, she no longer knew what the embrace meant.

Or what she wanted it to mean.

Brett didn't know why he continued to hold Caitlin close, why he wasn't quite ready to let her go.

Maybe because he appreciated the way she fit into his arms, the way her breasts pressed against his chest. Or maybe he hadn't yet had his fill of her intoxicating piña colada scent.

The silk of her hair lay soft against his cheek, and without a conscious thought, his lips brushed the strands in a whisper-soft kiss that was too inappropriate to contemplate, too out of line for anyone's good.

With her arms still locked around him, she lifted her head, her face, her eyes. And a vibrant aquamarine gaze wrapped around him like seaweed in the surf.

His heart slammed into his chest.

Should he apologize? Make some moronic excuse for letting a hug get out of hand?

He tried to think of an apology, an excuse, some explanation of why his body had taken charge of his brain—until he spotted desire brewing in her eyes, until her lips parted. And in the scheme of things, reason and good sense no longer seemed to matter. So he lowered his mouth to hers.

It was only a kiss, he told himself. No big deal. Something they could put behind them later, after their curiosity had been sated.

But as his tongue explored every wet, velvety nook and cranny of her mouth, tasting her sugar-and-cream sweetness, his blood soared, and he was lost in a swirl of testosterone and heat.

His hands caressed her back, memorizing each gentle curve. He had a half-assed wish that she'd pull away, make it easy on him. But she merely leaned into him and allowed the kiss to deepen.

Oh, damn. This wasn't a good idea.

But he gripped her hips and pulled her flush against his erection, a move that sent his hormones raging, a move that should have caused her to pull back, to withdraw.

Instead, she whimpered and threaded her fingers through the short strands of his hair.

The room began to spin, increasing his arousal, kicking it up a dangerous notch and threatening to pull him into the murky depths of something heavy.

Something he wasn't ready for.

A promise he couldn't make—not to a single

mother who held firm to a white-picket-fence dream, a dream she and her daughter deserved.

Something Kelly and Justin already had.

Damn. What in the hell had gotten into him? Home and hearth wasn't in the cards for a fly-boy like him—no matter how his temporary neighbor had turned his solo life upside down in a few short days.

With both fear and regret, he pulled his mouth from hers, breaking the kiss, ending the embrace, leaving his arms empty.

He raked a hand through his hair, as though the move might sort through his thoughts, stir up the right words.

The only ones that came to mind were, "I'm sorry about that."

"So am I." She took a deep breath, then blew it out. "God knows I don't need to get involved in a relationship right now."

A part of him wanted to know why not, to quiz her and find out what Gerald had been talking about. But the rebel in him clammed up. He couldn't allow the intimacy, the self-disclosure. Not if he wanted to survive the three-week house-sitting stint he'd signed on for.

And as much as he hated to admit it, he'd grown to care for the mother and child—too much.

He shoved his hands in the pockets of his shorts. "I'm glad we're on the same wavelength."

Still, the awareness, the attraction that had been brewing ever since the first day he'd laid eyes on her hadn't abated. And he feared, if given the chance, he'd kiss her again. How stupid was that?

"Well," he said, trying to put things on an even keel. "I'd better head home and check on those kittens."

It was the only excuse he could come up with, since his other reasons for escaping were too heavy to discuss.

"I'll see you tomorrow," she said, reminding him of the hold she had on him.

He nodded, then let himself out.

When the door closed behind him, he sucked in a lungful of the night breeze like a drowning man gulping for air, then he blew out a ragged breath.

He'd better start avoiding Caitlin and Emily whenever possible. It was the only way to distance himself.

Unfortunately, that would be a lot easier to pull off if he hadn't promised Emily she could visit "her" kittens tomorrow.

Chapter Six

Two days later, Brett sat on the sofa in Greg's condo, watching a baseball game on TV. The Padres were up three to one at the bottom of the sixth, and if luck and talent played out, they'd soon be on their way to the playoffs.

While the fans in the new Petco Park stadium took part in the seventh inning stretch, the TV station cut to a commercial. So Brett took his own time-out to grab a bag of chips from the cupboard and pull an ice-cold Corona from the fridge.

He'd stocked up on food since moving in, picking up the basic four food groups: meat, sweets, chips and beer. Before he could make it back to the couch, the telephone rang, and he snatched the receiver. "Hello."

"Greg Norse?" a man asked.

"No. He's not here. Can I help you?"

"This is Sam Crandall down at the Bayside Animal Shelter. Earlier this morning, a woman brought in a stray black cat that she found in the shrubs by her house off Maplewood Drive. A scan of the microchip gave us Mr. Norse's name and number. Looks like we've got his cat, Fred."

Brett glanced at the blue, carpet-covered cat house on stilts near the dining room window, where the kittens dozed in the late-afternoon sun. He blew a sigh out of one side of his mouth.

Finding Fred was good news, since he wouldn't have to tell Greg his beloved pet had run off or died. But what in the hell was Brett going to do with three cats when he hadn't even wanted one?

"I…uh…" he looked at the television, at the game that determined who would go to the playoffs.

"We close in thirty minutes," Mr. Crandall added. "And I'm sure Fred would like to spend the night at his own house."

Yeah—until the crotchety cat came home and found two new kittens had taken over his litter box, his food dish and his toys.

Then the fur was going to fly.

Brett blew out another sigh, this one loaded with resignation. "I'll come down there now."

"Good. I'm sure Fred will be happy to see a familiar face."

Brett didn't believe that for a minute; Fred hated him. Of course, Crandall didn't know that—yet.

He put the beer back in the fridge, took one last moment to watch the first couple of pitches, then grabbed his keys from the counter and headed to the carport.

Just as he climbed into the Explorer, he paused, remembering the shelter policy about taking animals home in a carrier. So he jogged back to the house for the cardboard box he'd been forced to buy.

He might be stuck with three cats, but he wasn't going to get stuck paying another ten bucks.

Fifteen minutes later, Brett arrived at the shelter and carried the empty cardboard carrier inside.

The clerk at the desk looked up, and by the name on his badge, Brett realized it was the guy who'd called.

"I came to get Fred," Brett said, as he placed the box on the counter.

"Good. I'll have him brought out. Our veterinary technician looked him over, but you might want to take him to his own vet tomorrow. It appears as though he's had a rough couple of days. We pulled out quite a few foxtails and gave him a flea dip. But he's got a tender spot on his left hip, and we're not sure what happened to his tail."

"What's wrong with the tail?"

"Looks like he got the tip of it caught or else something got a hold of it. But it ought to heal just fine." Crandall smiled and crossed his arms over a couch-potato belly. "Lucky for you someone brought him in."

Brett didn't feel lucky. He was still thinking about

how those cats were going to get along. He could buy another litter box and keep them in separate rooms, he supposed.

Crandall picked up the phone and, using an intercom system, called for number twenty-three to be brought to the front. Minutes later, a middle-age woman in uniform brought a subdued black cat through the door, taking care not to bump the wounded end of its tail.

The cat was pretty mellow.

Was it really Fred?

If a data-processing error occurred, the microchip might be wrong.

Too bad Brett hadn't brought Emily with him to make the official ID, but when he spotted the cat's yellow eyes, the tiny white spot on its chin, he had to believe the prodigal cat had returned.

Poor critter. He looked scared. Worn out.

For the first time since arriving at Greg's house, Brett actually sympathized with the cat. But he still worried Fred might freak out upon recognizing him, so he shoved the box forward. "Let's put him in here."

"All right." The woman carefully placed Fred in the container and closed the lid.

"I'll need you to sign this paper," Crandall said. "And I'll need thirty-five dollars."

"What's the money for?" Brett asked.

"It's the fee we charge for processing strays and returning them to their rightful owners."

"That ought to be a community service." Brett was getting tired of being hit with a fee or a charge every time he walked into this place. They seemed to be taking advantage of pet owners. Or, in his case, guilty cat-sitters.

"Sorry, sir. Just doing my job."

Brett paid the money, and in a matter of minutes, carried pesky Fred to the Explorer.

Trouble was, he found it hard to blame the cat for any of this. After all, in less than a week, his owner had disappeared, a stranger had moved in, a hyper-active terrier with a Napoleon complex had chased him through his house, and then God only knew what had terrorized him on the streets or in the canyon.

"Rough go of it?" he asked the feline.

Fred meowed, as though trying to talk, to tell Brett all about it. To say, "Let's get the hell out of here and go home."

But Brett didn't have the heart to forewarn the cat about his new roommates.

As he pulled into the complex, he spotted Caitlin returning home from work. She opened the car door, slid from the driver's seat and flashed him a warm smile. Just looking at her, even in white nurse shoes, baggy green pants and a medical shirt, took his breath away. But he regrouped and rolled down the window. "Guess who I have."

As she made her way toward him, he got out of the Explorer and reached for the box on the passenger seat.

"Is it Fred?" she asked, closing the gap between them until he caught the scent of a coconut-laced tropical breeze.

"One and the same."

She grinned and tucked a strand of hair behind her ear. "That's good news. Emily is going to be happy to hear that."

"I know. But now I have a houseful of cats."

"Better you than me." She grinned and tapped her nose with a finger. "The allergies, remember?"

"Yeah, I do." And that's why Brett was now responsible for three cats instead of one. Of course, he could have put his foot down, could have let Emily leave the animal shelter empty-handed that day. But the little blond pixie had a way of making him weak, especially when her eyes welled with tears.

"Emily has been *so* worried about Fred," Caitlin said, as they walked across the lawn to their respective front doors. "In fact, she's going to want to visit him this evening."

Hey, maybe that wasn't such a bad idea. With Emily's help, Fred might settle in better and accept the new kittens.

Brett shifted the box in his arms. "I was planning to throw a steak on the grill tonight. Why don't I put on a couple more, and you and Emily can join me for dinner."

"That sounds really nice," she said. "But I'm afraid I'd be sniffling and sneezing before I took one bite."

Oh, yeah. The damn allergies.

But another idea struck. "What if we eat outside on the patio? You can enter through the rear gate."

"That'll work." She flashed him a smile. "Can I bring something? A tossed salad maybe?"

"Sure. Sounds good." Of course, if they were going to get fancy, he'd better throw a couple of potatoes in the oven. And clean off the patio table. Maybe take a shower, too. "Give me about an hour, okay?"

"Sure. We'll see you then."

He stood on his porch and watched as she strode toward the Blackstone's to pick up her daughter. But when she glanced over her shoulder and caught him gaping at her, he grappled with the key and let himself in.

As he closed the door and prepared to set Fred free, a wave of apprehension struck. And not just because of the cat.

For a guy who'd made up his mind to avoid his pretty neighbor, he'd sure set himself up for another rush of temptation.

But it was too late to backpedal on a dinner invitation now.

For reasons Caitlin wouldn't contemplate, she showered, fussed a little too much with her hair and put on lipstick.

All the while, she made excuses for her behavior, like it had been a rough day at work and she and Emily didn't get out much. But the fact was she wanted to look attractive for her neighbor.

As she stood near the kitchen sink and tossed the salad with a homemade vinaigrette dressing, Emily entered the room.

"Mommy, it's five-five-nine. Can we please go see Fred now?"

Brett had said an hour, and it had only been about forty-five minutes. But Emily was so eager to see the runaway cat that Caitlin hated to make her wait any longer. "Sure, baby. We can go now."

"Goodie!"

Caitlin carried the bowl in one arm and grabbed a bottle of Merlot from the cupboard with the other. "Okay, Em. You lead the way."

Minutes later, they stood on the porch, and Emily rang the bell. By the way Caitlin's pulse was humming, she realized she was as eager to be here as her daughter. And that wasn't a good sign. Not if she meant to keep things between her and Brett simple and friendly.

She reminded herself that this wasn't a date. It was a neighborly barbecue. And a way to make Fred feel better about his house-sitter and his new roommates.

Brett opened the door, wearing a pair of jeans and a black T-shirt.

He'd showered since she'd seen him in the parking lot, just as she had. And he'd applied aftershave, even though she suspected he hadn't shaved. She kind of liked that rugged, lightly bristled look. It gave him an exciting edge that caused her senses to remain on high alert.

His eyes glimmered, and his lips curled in a smile. "Hi."

"I hope we're not too early, but Emily was eager to see Fred." She handed him the bottle of Merlot. "I'm not sure if you'd like wine this evening, but I thought we could have a glass while the steaks grill."

"Great." He took the wine, but his gaze swept over her again, warming her blood and sending it on a zippity-do-dah course through her body.

"We'll go around and enter through the backyard," she told him.

"But wait." Emily pressed forward and peered inside the door. "Where's Fred?"

Brett bent down on one knee to address her daughter, a move that surprised her. And pleased her. "As soon as I brought him home from the shelter and let him out of the carrier, he went into Greg's room and climbed under the bed. Why don't you go tell him you're here."

"All right." Emily dashed off to find the cat she thought of as a friend.

"How's Fred doing?" Caitlin asked. "Is he accepting the kittens?"

"I'm not sure he even knows they're here. He's been hiding for the past forty-five minutes." He clicked his tongue. "You know, the day he ran off, he'd just started to come out into the open, and now it looks as though he's had a setback."

"Fred really likes Emily, so I'm sure he'll be happy to see her."

"You know," he said, leaning against the doorjamb in a rebellious stance, "I've always liked dogs and never had much use for cats, but I feel kind of sorry for Fred. It wasn't until I picked him up at the pound that I realized what he'd gone through."

She tossed him a playful smile. "So the staunch dog lover has had a change of heart?"

"I wouldn't say that. I just hope the poor little guy doesn't suffer any lasting trauma from his days on the run. I think he lost a few of his lives, along with a bit of his tail."

"He lost a part of his tail?"

"Just the tip. I think those coyotes nearly caught him. But then, your guess is as good as mine."

They stood there, the threshold separating them. The conversation holding them. Or was it more than that? A push/pull neither of them was ready to admit, let alone deal with.

He flashed her a heart-stopping smile, then nodded toward the kitchen. "Why don't I meet you on the patio. I'll put the salad in the refrigerator, open the wine and bring out two glasses."

"Sounds good." She handed him the bowl, then walked around to the small backyard patio.

This dinner was beginning to feel more and more like a real date, in spite of her determination to keep things platonic between them.

And that couldn't possibly be good.

She unlatched the lock on the wrought iron gate, let herself into the small patio and took a seat in one of the plastic chairs Greg had purchased from a parking lot sale at the grocery store.

Moments later, Brett walked out the sliding door with two glasses of red wine. As he set one before her, his musky, sea-breeze scent nearly took her breath away.

"Thank you."

"You're welcome."

He pulled out a chair and joined her at the table. "Emily is patiently trying to coax Fred out from under the bed. She's trying to reason with him, if you can believe that. I've never seen a kid who loves animals like she does."

"Neither have I. If I didn't have an allergy to dander, I'd let her have a pet in a heartbeat."

"And I'd let her have two kittens, too. Free. I'd even throw in a cardboard carrier and wouldn't back charge you the two-hundred and thirty dollars I paid to get them sprung from the kitty slammer." He slid her a teasing smile that sent her heart topsy-turvy.

What was wrong with her? She had to get a grip on her emotional response to him. So in spite of a godawful urge to stare, to consider something neither of them wanted, she decided to keep the conversation light and easy. "By the way, Gerald said he's going to take you to the V.F.W. hall sometime soon."

"I know. We talked about it at the luau. He thinks I'd enjoy having a beer and shooting the breeze with some of the veterans."

"Would you?" she asked.

A grin tugged at one side of his mouth, and his blue eyes glimmered. "Yeah, I'd like that."

"Gerald is a nice man. And he's well liked in the neighborhood. Greg told me he's a war hero and was awarded a Purple Heart, a Silver Star and several other commendations during the Korean War."

"Interesting," Brett said. "I didn't realize that."

"Gerald's pretty tight-lipped about his military service, but one of the other veterans told Greg."

Brett leaned back in his seat, took a slow sip of wine and eyed her over the rim of his glass. "Gerald mentioned things are going to get hairy for you in the near future, but he didn't say why. What's up?"

She wasn't sure whether she should go into detail about the upcoming custody hearing. Not after learning about the nightmare he'd been through as a kid. But this fight was different. Caitlin was protecting her child, not her own selfish interests.

Besides, Brett had become a friend over the past week. And maybe she could share a bit of what she was up against.

"I'm Emily's foster mother," she told him.

His brow twitched at the news. "That's…surprising. You look so much alike. And you're so…maternal."

"I love her as if I'd given birth to her myself. As far as I'm concerned, I *am* her mother. And I'll do anything I can to protect her and keep her safe."

"For what it's worth, I think you're one of the best mothers I've ever seen."

His praise meant a lot, more than it should, and she reached for a smile. "I hope the court feels the same way. I'd love to adopt her."

"You've got my vote," he said.

"Thanks."

A lot depended upon the judge, but the fact Brett had confidence in her, as a mother, was uplifting.

Did she dare tell him the rest? About the custody battle? About her decision to fight Zack with everything she had?

"I can't see why the adoption wouldn't go

through," he said. "But I'd be happy to be a character witness, if you need one."

But would he be willing to speak on her behalf during a custody hearing?

After what he'd gone through as a child, he might not be willing to go to court and support her.

But maybe, if she explained...well, not everything. Just some of the reasons why she'd taken a stand.

She glanced across the table, caught his eye. "When I was a child, the courts found my mother negligent and placed me in foster care for most of my growing-up years. Some homes were better than others. And when I turned eighteen, I decided that as soon as I had a stable job and a home, I'd apply with the county and become a foster mother myself. I wanted to provide a child with the love I never had."

"Emily is lucky to have been placed in your home, Caitlin."

"Thank you, but I'm the lucky one. She's blessed my life in more ways than you can ever imagine."

"How long have you had her?"

"Since birth. Her mother was pregnant and an innocent victim of a drive-by shooting. She was rushed by ambulance to the hospital, where just an hour before she died, the doctors delivered Emily by an emergency caesarian section."

"That's too bad."

Caitlin nodded. "Emily was three weeks early, but healthy and beautiful. And when the pediatrician released her from the hospital nursery, a social worker brought her to my house." Caitlin smiled, remembering the day her daughter had been placed in her arms. "I named her Emily Joy for the happiness she brought into my life."

"I assume there weren't any other family members who wanted her," Brett said.

"No. Her mother had come to the San Diego area as a teenage runaway and had lived on the streets much of the time. She'd finally turned her life around through Lydia House, a program run by the Park Avenue Community Church. She had a job and was taking some classes at the junior college, but there was no one to take the baby."

"So why do I get the feeling you're worried about the adoption not going through without a hitch?"

"Because her biological father refused to sign the papers." She wondered how much more to reveal, how much to tell him, especially since they were just steps away from the open screen door. But since Emily wasn't near the kitchen or within hearing distance, she relaxed a bit.

As she pondered her words, though, the enormity of her dilemma struck a hard blow to the chest, and the fear of losing Emily made it difficult to breathe, to speak.

The child she loved with all her heart might be ripped from her arms and placed with a convicted felon, a man who'd taken part in an armed robbery that left a man paralyzed from a bullet in the back.

Before she could respond, a tear slipped down her face. And then another.

Brett had never been able to handle a woman's

tears, especially one as sweet and damn near perfect as Caitlin. He reached across the small table and caught the warm droplet with his thumb. "Don't cry. It'll be okay."

She lifted her face and smiled through her tears, as though appreciating his strength, his understanding.

Something began to swirl between them, gaining speed and heat, drawing him to her. He cupped her jaw, and his thumb caressed her cheek.

God help him, he was going to kiss her again.

But before he could move, Emily shouted happily from the kitchen. "Guess what!"

His hand dropped to the table with a guilty thud, and they both jerked back in their seats, like school-kids caught doing something wrong.

Emily opened the screen and stepped onto the patio, her eyes lit up, her excitement apparent. "Fred came out from under the bed."

"That's good," Brett said.

"I know," she told him. "But I had to promise to never ever bring Scruffy to visit him again. And I told him that we loved him very much, and that he had to come out so you would know he was a good cat and not a sycold one."

Neither Brett nor Caitlin corrected her reference to his earlier "psycho cat" comment. In fact, neither of them spoke at all. Apparently, whatever had been going on between them still churned in the air.

"Now Fred is meeting Fluffy and Princess," Emily said, "but I have to hurry back so I can help them be friends." Then she disappeared into the house, leaving the adults alone again.

An awkwardness settled over Brett. And over Caitlin, too, he suspected. He watched as she fiddled with the stem of her wineglass.

It was as though they hadn't broached intimacy, as though they hadn't touched, hadn't silently acknowledged the desire that brewed under the surface. And he wasn't sure whether he was sorry or not.

Maybe it was a good time to start the grill.

He took one last drink of wine, one last look at the pretty woman who sat across from him.

Her blond hair was all soft and glossy this evening, as it brushed against her shoulders. And her expression bore a vulnerability he hadn't spotted before.

He almost wished he could break his no-dating-single-moms rule, especially since he'd already held one in his arms, already tasted her kiss.

But instead of saying—or doing—something stupid, he pushed his chair away from the table and stood. This dinner was becoming a little too heavy for his own good.

He knew better than to get involved in a romantic relationship with Caitlin, no matter how much his libido argued differently.

She and her daughter deserved more than a guy who would flit in and out of their lives.

As he turned on the grill and lit the flame, he vowed to keep his hands to himself for the rest of the evening, even if it killed him.

But when he stole another glance at his pretty neighbor, saw the silky strands of her hair, the dusky pink of her parted lips, the vast blue Pacific of her eyes, he realized holding to a vow of celibacy and friendship would probably do him in.

This was going to be one hell of a long night.

Chapter Seven

As the sun set over Bayside and the Ocean Breeze condominiums, Brett sat at the patio table, leaned back in his seat and studied his pretty blond dinner companion.

Not only was Caitlin a pleasure to look at, but she was a good cook, too.

Okay, so she'd only contributed the tossed salad. But the dressing—it had to be some secret recipe—was out of this world.

He wondered how long it would take another man to give up a life-long habit of fast food and take-out. Or how long it would take a guy who actually wanted to set down roots to start shopping for diamond rings.

Not long, he suspected.

"The steak was really good," she said.

"So was your salad."

She smiled and fiddled with the sheet of paper towel he'd given her to use as a napkin.

They hadn't broached the subject of the tear she'd shed in front of him or the kiss that almost occurred—probably because Emily's happy mealtime chatter had kept adult thoughts and desire at bay. But after the little girl had asked her mother to be excused and went back inside to play with the cats, the sexual awareness returned in a slow and steady rush.

And for the life of him, Brett wasn't sure what he wanted to do about it. Reach across the table and take her hand? Come right out and ask how she felt about a natural progression to sex—no strings attached, of course?

Or should he run like hell?

She folded the paper towel as though it were linen and placed it on her plate. "Thanks for inviting us over this evening. Emily and I don't get out much, and it was nice not having to cook on a work night."

He ought to be glad that she'd made the decision for them both.

And he was.

But that didn't still the quiet voice of disappointment, the feeling that something special had slipped through his fingers like liquid gold.

Let it go, he told himself, forcing a casual smile. "I'm glad you came. Emily has been a big help with the cats. I'm not sure I could have ever talked Fred out from under the bed."

"She was happy to help. This has been a special and exciting day for her."

Before he could respond, the bright-eyed pixie ran into the kitchen and peered through the sliding door screen. "Mommy, can you please come inside for just a little minute and see Fred and Princess and Fluffy?"

Caitlin smiled. "All right, honey."

When the child ran back toward the living room, Brett leaned forward and rested his forearms on the table. "What about your allergies?"

She gave a half shrug. "You have no idea how much I enjoy sharing in her excitement. So I'll go inside until my eyes start watering and I'm overcome by a flurry of sneezes. Then at home, I'll take an allergy pill to deal with the congestion."

In spite of knowing better, he ran a knuckle along her cheek. "Like I said, you're one hell of a mom."

"Thanks. And you're a nice friend and neighbor." She flashed him an appreciative grin, then cleared the patio table of dirty plates and silverware and carried them into the kitchen.

But Brett didn't jump up. He just sat there, struggling with the word "nice."

She'd meant it as a compliment, he supposed. And it ought to be a relief and a comfort to know she wasn't making things more complicated between them. But the word "nice" had never sat well with him, especially now. And he'd be damned if he knew why.

But he shook it off, recorked what was left of the wine and carried the bottle and glasses into the house.

As Caitlin started to fill the sink with soap and water, he stopped her. "I'll wash the dishes after you go home."

"All right. But it'll be easier if they soak for a while." She turned off the faucet and dried her hands. "Let's go see those kittens."

He led the way to the living room, where Emily sat on the floor with the cats—all three of them.

It wasn't as though Fred had joined in the kitty fun and games, but he perched himself on the armrest of the sofa and observed from a safe distance, as though he knew better than to get too close, too chummy. Too attached.

Interesting. Brett could relate to being curious about his new neighbors, drawn into their lives by fate. Held back by a sense of reason and self-protection.

As Caitlin took a seat on the edge of the sofa, Brett chose the side nearest Fred. He expected the cat to scamper back to the bedroom, like he'd done in the past whenever Brett had approached. But Fred merely looked at him in a what's-a-guy-supposed-to-do? way.

I hear you, buddy. Brett slowly lifted his hand and stroked the cat's black fur, felt the rumble of a purr.

Well, what do you know? He and Fred had reached a truce, an understanding, a respect for each other.

"Look at them." Caitlin nodded to the floor where Emily sat with the two kittens.

He couldn't remember which one was Princess and which one was Fluffy, but the orange tabby suddenly pounced on the head of the gray kitten, and they began to wrestle using their little teeth and paws.

Emily giggled and clapped her hands. "Aren't they funny?"

"They sure…uh…uh…" Caitlin lifted a finger to her nose, blinked her eyes and covered her mouth. "Uh-choo."

"Bless you," Brett said.

"Thank you." She sniffled, then looked at him with red, watery eyes and sneezed again.

And again.

"Well," she said, "I guess it's time for us to leave."

"Do we have to?" Emily asked.

"I'm afraid so." Caitlin stood and looked at Brett. "Thanks again for dinner."

"You're welcome." He got to his feet and walked his neighbor and her daughter to the door. As he let them out, he had half a notion to give them each a hug goodbye, but he knew better than that.

Still, he stood in the doorway and watched them cut across the lawn to their front porch.

Mother and child.

When they were halfway home, Emily turned and gave him a little wave, sending his thoughts tumbling. And without warning, loneliness broadsided him, his memories taking a direct hit.

His first day back in San Diego. The drive out to Periwinkle Lane. Watching Justin run down the street, leap over the small hedge in front of his house and yell, "Mom, I'm home."

His boy, his son.

A child he didn't even know.

His heart knotted into a lump, and the urge to

reach out and pick up the telephone, struck him full-force.

Call Kelly.

Ask about Justin.

Tell her you want to meet him, that you want to be a small part of his life.

But after five years of not speaking, what would she say if he called out of the blue?

She'd probably flip. Raise her voice. Ask him who the hell he thought he was to come prancing into their lives on a whim.

But this wasn't a whim; it was a full-on internal battle he'd been waging for years.

He swore under his breath.

So what should he do? Succumb to emotional weakness and call Kelly tonight? Or did he leave her and Justin in peace, like he'd always done?

For a guy who'd always been decisive, who'd sworn he'd walk away from a child of his own before subjecting him to custody disputes, Brett wasn't so sure anymore.

He could sure use some fatherly advice, but not the counsel of his own dad, a man who'd retired and moved to Phoenix with his new wife years ago.

So he picked up the cordless telephone and dialed Harry's number.

The retired detective who'd become more than a friend picked up on the second ring. "Hello."

Just the sound of his voice was soothing.

"Harry, it's Brett. How's it going?"

"At my age, if I felt any better, I'd have to see a

doctor and have a slew of tests run." Harry chuckled at his own joke. "How's the Navy treating you, son?"

Son.

Brett would never get used to the rush of pride he felt when Harry called him son. "I'm doing just fine. But I've got a question I want to ask you."

"Shoot."

"I…uh…know you didn't agree with my decision to pull out of Justin's life years ago, but I did what I thought was best at the time."

"I know you did."

"And you told me I might be sorry later."

"I had a feeling you would."

"Well, you were right. I'd like to call Kelly and set up a visit, but I'm not sure how she'll react. Things ended badly the last time we talked, and even though I've always been prompt with child support payments, she's never thanked me or contacted me."

Had his ex-wife lied to the boy? Told him that David was his father? Would she resent Brett's interference?

"How long has it been?" Harry asked.

"Since I saw Justin? Five years."

"You're his father, Brett. And you've been paying more than your fair share of child support. Legally, she can't keep him away from you."

Legally. That meant a judge, attorneys. Fights. Painful disruptions to the life of an innocent little boy.

Brett raked a hand through his hair. "I don't want to go through the courts."

"Your ex-wife probably doesn't, either. I bet she'd be willing to compromise."

Brett wasn't so sure. During the short time they'd been married, he and Kelly had never been able to compromise on anything. Why would she be agreeable now?

He was afraid to hope she might welcome him back into her and Justin's lives without a squawk. "What if she isn't willing to let me see him and I'm not willing to get an attorney involved?"

"Then you'll have to let things ride and hope you're not doing your son a bigger disservice by not being a part of his life."

"Dammit." Brett gripped the receiver in his hand until his knuckles ached. "You're supposed to make me feel better, not worse."

"Listen, son. I've got to call it the way I see it. Don't forget about the trouble I had finding my daughter Hailey. And how great it's been for all of us, now that we've been able to work through the problems of the past."

Yeah. Brett knew about the illegitimate daughter Harry had fathered during the time he and Kay had been separated. And he knew about Harry's search to find her, a search that took years and didn't pan out until she was an adult. "How's Hailey doing?"

"Great. She and Nick are having a baby girl in September, and they couldn't be happier. Kay's been helping her decorate the nursery. And I've been refinishing an old rocker that once belonged to my grandmother."

"How's Nick holding up?" Brett asked.

"He couldn't be better." Harry laughed. "The man

actually walks around with a smile on his face half the time." Harry laughed.

"That's good." Brett had always liked Nick Granger—maybe because they were both loners. And the fact that they both had been one of the guys Harry had befriended gave them even more in common.

"So," Harry said, "let's get back to your question. It won't hurt for you to give Kelly a call and ask to see your son."

Brett wasn't so sure about that. But he figured Harry was right, like he'd usually proven to be, even if Brett hadn't always taken his advice. "Thanks, Harry. I'll give it some thought."

"By the way, I'm glad you're back in town. Kay and I are throwing a barbecue at the beach this Friday. We're inviting all the guys, although I'm not sure who will show up. We'd love to have you join us."

Over time, Brett had become a part of Harry's extended family, which included about a dozen guys who credited the retired detective with helping them succeed when their teenage choices had them racing down the wrong path at breakneck speed.

"Sounds great," Brett told him.

"We've got at least one other guy bringing a kid," Harry added. "So feel free to bring your son, if you'd like."

Brett couldn't think of anything he'd like more than taking Justin to meet Harry and the guys. But using an invitation to a barbecue at the beach wasn't a good enough excuse to call his ex after all these years.

Besides, his son didn't even know him. And Kelly wouldn't let him just drive up and take the boy with him.

No, taking Justin to the beach party was out of the question until Brett and Kelly had a chance to talk, to strike some kind of bargain, to work out visitation.

"Joe Davenport just met the son he didn't know he had," Harry said. "So I'm sure he can give you a few pointers. It didn't take them very long to bond."

That was nice to know. But Brett couldn't take Justin to this beach party on Friday. It was too soon.

But you can take Emily, a small voice said. *She and her mom don't get out very much. And she'd probably like going to the beach, building a sand castle, playing in the shallow waves.*

"What do you think?" Harry asked.

"I may give Kelly a call later this week. Maybe she'll let me take Justin next time." He took a deep breath and slowly blew it out. "But I've got a neighbor who has a little girl. Would it be all right if I brought them?"

"Of course. The more the merrier. Why don't you pick up some fried chicken or something. And maybe a six-pack of beer or soda."

"You got it," he told Harry. But knowing Caitlin, he figured she'd want to cook something—something that would taste a heck of a lot better than a bucket of fried chicken that had sat under heat lamps for too long.

"We're meeting at Playa Del Sol, the same beach where we had that party the last time you were in town. Kay and I are going to arrive early and try to get the fire ring that's near the volleyball court, but I don't think anyone else will show up before five or five-thirty."

"All right. I'll see you then."

"Great. I'm looking forward to it."

"Me, too." When the line disconnected, and Brett hung up the receiver, he sat back in his chair and studied the telephone.

It was too late to call Kelly tonight. At least, that's the excuse he made.

But should he give Caitlin a call now or wait until morning?

Caitlin had been surprised when Brett invited them to the beach party and had almost declined, since she'd been scheduled to work this afternoon. But knowing how much fun Emily would have, she'd called a co-worker and switched days with her.

While waiting for Brett to arrive, she scanned the contents of the two canvas tote bags she'd packed for the beach party, hoping she had everything they would need. She had towels, sun block, sand toys, a change of clothes for Emily, sweatshirts for them both, a first-aid kit for any unexpected emergency. That ought to do it.

And in a cooler, she had ice, drinking water, a pasta salad and homemade peanut butter cookies. As far as she was concerned, she and Emily were ready to go.

Of course, Emily had been ready before noon,

when she'd put on her red polka dot bathing suit—
just in case Brett arrived earlier than five.

And to be honest, Caitlin had been filled with anticipation, too. But she'd waited until four-thirty to
put on her beach attire.

She glanced down at the pair of white shorts she
wore to cover the black bikini, which was more conservative than most. Or so she'd convinced herself.

Maybe she should have worn a different cover-up,
like an oversize shirt. But she admonished herself for
feeling self-conscious. This was just a casual get together at the beach, a potluck with Brett's friends, the
Logans.

Still, when the doorbell rang, she struggled with
both a growing feminine awareness and a soaring
sense of excitement.

"I'll get it," Emily said, as she dashed for the door,
her flip-flops snapping and flapping across the hardwood floor.

Caitlin followed behind her daughter, that sense
of awareness and anticipation mounting. As the door
swung open, Emily greeted Brett. "We're all ready
to go to the beach party."

"Good." He smiled at the child, until he spotted
Caitlin, and his expression sobered in a sexual way.

Her pulse rate skittered, as his gaze swept the
length of her, then leaped into overdrive when his
eyes lingered at breast-level.

When his gaze lifted and locked on hers, a full-
bodied, hot-blooded burst of carnal energy nearly
took her breath away.

He seemed to recover quicker than she did, and his lips quirked in a crooked grin. "If I had known how good you look in a bikini, I would have invited you to go swimming sooner."

Her heart took flight at the compliment, and she struggled with a response.

Was a thank-you in order? Or should she downplay the remark?

Oh, for goodness sake. They'd both decided this relationship was destined to remain platonic.

Emily tugged at the hem of Brett's white T-shirt. "I was ready for a long, long time. And it's only four-four-nine. Do we still have to wait?"

He grinned and gently stroked the top of her head. "I'm tired of watching the clock, too. We can go now, if it's okay with your mom."

"That's fine with me. I'm ready." Caitlin nodded at her bags and the cooler. "Will you help me carry these to the car?"

"Of course," he said, chuckling. "It looks like you even included the kitchen sink."

"Everything but," she said. "I like to be prepared, that's all."

"I had a feeling you would." He grinned, eyes twinkling with mirth, then placed the heaviest canvas bag on top of the ice chest and carried it to the car.

She grabbed the other one, slipped the strap of her purse over her shoulder and locked the house.

When they'd loaded the Explorer, Caitlin grabbed Brett by the arm. "Wait a minute."

"What's the matter? Did you forget something?"

She dropped her hand, but a connection remained—unseen, unspoken, but strong. She nibbled on her bottom lip and tried to think of a way to explain that she didn't know the Logans and felt a little uneasy with what she'd chosen to wear. "Maybe I ought to put on a blouse before we go."

"Don't you dare. I like what you're wearing. And I'm going to make sure you go out in the water, so I can see the rest of your suit." The appreciation in his grin taunted her in a good way, and a flood of feminine pride surged, challenging the conservative side she'd developed over the past four years.

"All right, let's go," she said, releasing whatever hold she'd had on him with a bit of reluctance and immediately feeling the loss.

What was with that?

Fortunately, Emily's presence diffused the awkwardness. The little girl chattered all the way to Playa Del Sol about the things she wanted to do at the beach, like building a castle that went all the way to the sky. And playing in the water.

By the time they parked in a lot adjacent to the beach, the sun had lowered over the Pacific, and the sea breeze stirred the scent of sand and salt water. As they climbed from the car, gulls cried out in welcome.

"There they are." Brett pointed to an older couple who'd set lawn chairs and blankets near a fire ring.

The gray-haired man appeared to be in his sixties, but was tall and powerfully built. His wife was probably a few years younger, petite and attractive.

Brett waved at the Logans, then helped Emily

from the car. "Caitlin, let me introduce you two, then I'll come back for our things."

They walked through the parking lot and onto the sand, with Emily striding ahead. When she stepped out of a flip-flop, she looked at Caitlin. "Uh-oh. My shoe."

While Caitlin stooped to pick up her daughter's sandal, Brett lifted the little girl in his arms and carried her the rest of the way.

Mrs. Logan, a rosy-cheeked woman with copper-colored hair, strode toward Brett. "We're so glad you're back in town."

With Emily still in his arms, Brett greeted the older lady with a hug and a kiss on the cheek. "Kay, you look just as pretty as ever."

"Thank you, dear." She placed a hand on Emily's arm and blessed her with a warm, grandmotherly smile. "Who is this pretty little girl?"

"This is Emily and her mother, Caitlin." He slipped an arm around Caitlin's waist, and although he held her lightly, the affectionate move sent a shimmy of warmth through her veins.

She struggled not to lean against him, not to slip her arm around him, too, and greeted Mrs. Logan instead. "How do you do?"

As Harry joined them, Brett continued the introductions.

The retired detective, who was just as gracious and welcoming as his wife, patted Brett on the back. "It's good to see you, son. And to meet your friends."

"Brett," Emily said, placing her little hand on his jaw. "When can we make the castle?"

He grinned at the eager child. "As soon as I get the things from out of the car. You wait here with your mommy."

Moments later, Brett returned, and Caitlin began to lay out a blanket on which they could sit and place their things. Emily quickly dug into the blue canvas tote and found her sand toys, as Brett shed his shirt.

Caitlin couldn't help but admire his broad shoulders, the corded muscles of his back and, when he turned, the light splatter of dark hair on his chest that narrowed as it disappeared under the waistband of a green surfer-style swimsuit.

As her scan reached his face, she caught his eye and realized he'd known she'd been looking at him, admiring his body. A flood of warmth rushed to her cheeks and her movements stilled, as words and excuses escaped her.

"Mommy, are you going to help us build the castle?" Emily asked.

"In a minute, honey." She nodded toward the blanket. "As soon as I finish unpacking."

Brett took Emily by the hand. "Come on, we'll find the perfect spot and start without your mom." He led her toward the water, where the sand was wet and solid.

When Caitlin had organized everything on their blanket, she couldn't help but watch from a distance, admiring Brett's physique as he helped Emily build a moat to protect their castle from the waves.

The man was real hero material, if you asked her.

Daddy and husband material, she suspected. And she was sorry they'd decided to keep things platonic. Sorry that she had to remain unattached until custody of Emily had been decided.

"For a man who tends to avoid children," Kay said, "Brett is certainly good with your daughter."

Caitlin tried to hide the surprise from her face. Brett certainly hadn't avoided Emily. Of course, her daughter had never given him a chance to.

She turned her attention to the older woman. "I had no idea he was uncomfortable around children. He's been great with Emily, and she adores him."

Brett had also been a wonderful neighbor, and she was growing to care a great deal for him. But she kept her personal thoughts and growing affection for the Navy helicopter pilot to herself.

"It does my heart good to see him happy," Kay said. "Of all Harry's boys, Brett has held a special place in my heart."

Caitlin wanted to ask why, but before she could, Harry spoke. "Well, look who's here."

The women turned toward the parking lot, where a blond couple and a towheaded little boy approached.

"It's the Davenports," Harry said, striding toward them.

Moments later, Caitlin was introduced to Joe Davenport, a tall, muscular man wearing a navy blue shirt with a Bayside Fire Department logo, his wife Kristin and their seven-year-old son, Bobby.

Kristin was a classy, stylishly dressed woman, tall

and willowy with golden brown hair and green eyes. She wore a linen shorts set. The blouse didn't hide a swell to her abdomen.

"Didn't you have that ultrasound today?" Kay asked.

Kristin shot a glance at her husband and grinned. Before they answered, Bobby spoke up. "I'm going to be a big brother to two babies."

Caitlin couldn't help but grin at the towheaded kid with a cowlick and a scatter of freckles across his nose who was obviously looking forward to being a big brother.

"That's wonderful news." Kay gave Kristin a hug. "You'll certainly have your hands full for a while. But what a blessing twins are going to be."

Joe slipped an arm around his wife. "She's going to have plenty of help with them. I didn't get a chance to be around Bobby when he was a baby, and I plan to make up for it this time around."

Harry and Kay's happiness for the Davenports was genuine, and Caitlin could easily see why the Logans had earned a special place in Brett's heart. She was drawn to them, too.

Joe took his son by the hand. "Come on, Bobby. I want to introduce you to a friend of mine. He's the guy helping the little girl build a sand castle. Maybe they'll let us help."

Caitlin smiled, as she watched the father and son join Emily and Brett.

Brett stood and shook hands with Joe, their smiles warm, their friendship and respect for each other apparent. But when Brett glanced at Bobby, he seemed to tense and stiffen.

Had Kay been right?

Was Brett uncomfortable around children?

Bobby plopped down in the sand next to Emily and the two began to work together in the sand, making quick friends, as children were prone to do.

But Caitlin watched Brett, watched his eyes. She sensed it was a struggle for him to look at the boy and a struggle not to.

What was going on?

She would have to talk to him about it later—if she could get him alone.

But for some reason, she had a feeling he'd welcome an escape right now.

Chapter Eight

Bobby Davenport was a cute kid, with wheat-colored hair, golden brown eyes and a freckled nose. It was easy to see that he favored his father, but just looking at the boy was killing Brett.

If Bobby had been wearing a pair of jeans, a white T-shirt and a red baseball cap, he'd look just like Justin had the day Brett had been watching from across the street, while seated on his Harley.

The two boys had to be about the same age. Did they have anything else in common? Maybe saving baseball cards and watching the same cartoons?

Conflicting emotions blindsided Brett, taunting him with an overwhelming compulsion to stare at the kid, to question him about things, like school and sports and video games. But at the same time, he had a pressing need to grab his keys from the top of Caitlin's blanket, make a mad dash to the car and put the pedal to the metal before weakness overcame him and he got all soft and teary-eyed in front of people.

Ever since Brett and Kelly had divorced, he'd dealt with his decision to walk away from Justin by steering clear of kids, especially little boys who reminded him of his son.

Like Bobby did.

As the boy dug in the sand with both hands, he glanced up and shot his father a broad smile, revealing a missing front tooth.

Had Justin lost any teeth yet? And if so, what was the tooth fairy's going rate these days? Shouldn't a dad know things like that?

"Hey." The sound of Caitlin's voice lured him away from the thoughts that would become self-destructive, if he continued to dwell on them.

He glanced over his shoulder, allowing the sight of the petite blond nurse to be a balm to his shattered emotions.

"We're making a castle," he told her, although his focus on the project had shifted the moment the seven-year-old boy with a cowlick dropped to his knees and began to form the base with a pile of sand.

"I can see that." She blessed him with another smile, this one loaded with something soft and genuine, feminine and alluring. "And you're doing a fine job of it."

He shrugged, ready for an escape—any escape, even the familiar but uncomfortable lure he felt whenever he was around her. It sure beat the hell out of thinking about Justin.

"Will you take a walk along the beach with me?" she asked. "Kay said she'd keep an eye on Emily."

"Uh, yeah. Sure." He stood and brushed at the sand on his knees and swim trunks.

"Brett and I won't be gone very long," she told her daughter. "Mrs. Logan said she'd watch you."

Emily, her hands and arms shoved deep into a bucket of sand and water, grinned. "Okay, Mommy. Joe is showing us how to make pretty little squiggles on the princess tower."

"I'll keep an eye on her, too," Joe volunteered. "It'll help me know what to expect if one of our babies turns out to be a girl."

"Thanks." Caitlin flashed him an appreciative grin, then turned her attention on Brett. She crossed her arms, forcing her breasts to swell out of the black material of her bikini top. "Are you ready?"

Way more than he ought to be, since he was jumping from one emotional powder keg to another. "Sure, let's go."

As they started down the shoreline, Brett didn't trust himself to talk, to ask where they were going. As it was, he just enjoyed the wet, squishy feel of water and sand on his bare feet, the salty kick to the breeze, the lonely cry of a seagull. And, when Caitlin didn't know he was stealing a glance at her, he especially enjoyed having the pretty blonde at his side.

She scanned the color-streaked horizon. "It's going to be a beautiful sunset."

He supposed it would be, although he'd never been one to get mushy or sentimental about things like that. But since it seemed to matter to her, he looked at the sky, saw the pink and orange tinted clouds as the sinking sun stretched them like streaks of paint on an easel. "You're right."

Her shoulder brushed against him once or twice, and each time he had an urge to take her hand, to slip an arm around her and pull her close. To make this walk on the beach into something it shouldn't be.

Hell, his emotions were going nuts today, and he was being bombarded with all kinds of unwelcome feelings that clawed at his chest.

"Brett," she said, drawing his rapt attention and making him wonder if she'd had some ulterior motive for getting him away from the others. "What was going on back there?"

Back where? At the sand castle? "I don't know what you mean."

She bent, picked up a striped shell, studied it a moment, then wiped it against her shorts before sticking it in her pocket. "Kay mentioned you avoid small children. I found that hard to believe, since you're so good to Emily. But then I watched you with Bobby. You appeared to tense as though you were uncomfortable."

He looked ahead, at the gulls that fought over the bright green paper that had once packaged a granola bar, at two men fishing off the jetty. At the setting sun that dipped behind an orange, silver-lined cloud. He really didn't want to discuss it with her, but he couldn't dispute what she'd seen or what she'd sensed. And he didn't want her to get the wrong idea about him and kids. It wasn't as though he didn't like them.

"I have a son I haven't seen in a long time," he admitted. "I'm not happy about the way things are, and being around kids is a real bummer. That's all."

"I'm sorry," she said.

For a moment he thought she might take his hand, offer him some kind of condolence. And he wasn't sure if that would be a good thing or not.

"How old is your son?"

That much he could tell her. "He's Bobby's age."

"I see."

Did she? He didn't think a woman like her with a maternal side as vast as the Pacific would understand why a man would walk away from his son, why he wouldn't put up a fight.

Brett might have convinced himself that he'd done the right thing five years ago, but his recent waffling made him less sure about the decision. And he'd be damned if he'd let her think of him as a loser dad. "It's a long and complicated story, and I don't want to get into it right now."

"If you ever want to talk about it, I'm a good listener." She slid him an understanding smile, a vibrant heart-tugging one that made him almost believe she'd see his side.

"Thanks." He returned a grin, but it wasn't anywhere near as upbeat as hers. Or nearly as hopeful.

He figured that was the end of the discussion, but

her gaze lingered on him, as though she was searching for the things he hadn't told her. But she didn't press him. Not with words.

Damn. He had to do something, had to change the subject, lift the mood. So he playfully bumped his arm against hers. "Let's go swimming."

"Here?" she asked, those sea-green eyes growing wide with disbelief.

"Why not?"

"We don't have towels."

He wondered if she ever temporarily chucked that motherly side and, hoping she would, slid her a taunting smile. "What are you—a woman or a mouse?"

"Throwing down the gauntlet, huh?" She laughed, then unbuttoned her shorts.

A gentleman might glance the other way, pretending disinterest in the unveiling. But Brett's rebel spirit wouldn't let him tear his eyes away. He watched as she slid the shorts down her hips, revealing a bikini-clad shape that could make a grown man stutter and stammer like a goofy adolescent suffering from a testosterone overload.

Damn. All along, he'd suspected she'd have a hot body, but the proof of it nearly took his breath away. Full breasts, a small taut waist, rounded hips, shapely legs.

And he knew, without a doubt, she'd look even better minus that sleek black material.

As she tossed her shorts onto the dry sand, he lassoed his libido—but just barely.

"Come on." He took her by the hand. "Last one in is a rotten egg."

They ran into the water like a couple of kids with no cares in the world.

He wasn't sure how long they laughed and played—long enough to know his attractive neighbor was more than someone's mom. Much more. She was a girl, a woman and a lady, all rolled into one small but dynamite package. A package barely held together by the strings of a black bikini.

As a wave approached, Brett dove underwater before it struck, and Caitlin followed. When he popped to the surface, he wiped his eyes with his hand and stole a glance at her, just as she cupped her hand and splashed him in the face.

"Hey," he said in a mock complaint.

She turned to run, sloshing through the thigh-high water, and he took off after her. The water slowed his steps, but his stride was longer than hers, and he closed the gap. When he was within arms' distance, he grabbed her, intending to catch her, to playfully retaliate, to get her back.

But as his hands clasped her waist, as she glanced over her shoulder and their eyes locked, sexual awareness slammed into him like a tsunami.

The passion that had been brewing under the surface rose to a head, and there was no damn way he could ignore the heat, ignore the desire to kiss her, to dip his tongue into her mouth, to run his hands along the curves of her bare skin.

He pulled her body to his, not at all sure what her

reaction would be. But instead of pushing him away, her hands slipped around his neck. She raised up on tiptoe and drew his mouth to hers—beating him to the punch.

He didn't usually do this sort of thing in public, but this stretch of the beach had been pretty deserted when they'd arrived. So he let himself go, falling into the spell she'd cast over him.

The kiss began slowly, tentatively, but as passion took the lead, tongues mated in a vigorous hunger, tasting, savoring, seeking.

But it was more than the sleek, wet inside of her mouth that Brett wanted to explore.

When was the last time a kiss had sent his hormones raging, his heart pounding, his blood racing like this? He'd be damned if he could remember. In fact, he doubted another woman's kiss had ever affected him like this, turning him every which way but loose.

His hands slid along her slick skin, laying claim to each tantalizing curve. Mere strings kept her from being naked, from being completely his.

Desire nearly knocked him to his knees. He wanted to make love, and it didn't matter where—in a bed, in the back seat of a car, on a patch of grass. Anywhere he could stretch alongside her and love her with his hands, his mouth, his body, taking her—taking them—someplace they'd never been. And he wouldn't stop until he was fully spent.

A wave built, and as it threatened to splash against them, especially her, he lifted her out of the way. Yet their kiss continued.

She wrapped her legs around his waist, the crotch of her bathing suit pressing against his belly, close to the tip of a demanding erection. Did she have any idea what she was doing to him?

The woman was driving him insane—and making him like it. A lot.

His fingers slid under the strap of her bikini top, and he stroked the swell of her breast.

She moaned into his mouth. Or was that an "uh-oh"? When she pulled her lips away, an "Oops" escaped.

"What's the matter?"

"Surfers at twelve o'clock."

He glanced over his shoulder and spotted a couple of teenage boys sitting on their boards, snickering.

Great. He and Caitlin had become adolescent entertainment.

"Sorry," he said. "I don't usually get carried away when there's an audience."

"Neither do I." But she didn't release him. Instead, she continued to hold him close, her arms clasped around his neck, her legs around his waist.

And for some dumb reason, he didn't give a squat what people thought. "This is crazy, Caitlin."

"I know." She rested her head against his, but still didn't unwrap her legs, didn't release her arms.

If it were already dark…if they were here alone… if…

He held her close enough to feel the beat of her heart. Or maybe that was his pulse beating in his head, reminding him he could use some relief, the heady kind that came from sexual release.

"So what are we going to do about it?" he asked, hoping she'd agree with his libido and want to satisfy their lust.

"I'm not sure." She took a deep breath, then slowly blew it out. "But I won't tell you that I don't feel anything, that I don't want to take things to a deeper level."

"Well, we damn sure can't do that here."

"I know." She slowly released her legs, allowing him to set her down.

"I guess we'd better head back to the party."

She nodded, and he took her by the hand and led her to the shore.

But the desire to make love with her was just as strong as it had ever been. And the thought of taking her to bed lingered in his mind, long after she put on her shorts and they headed back to the fire ring.

Caitlin had no idea what the others thought when she and Brett returned looking like a couple of rats that had barely escaped a sinking ship.

Of course, since everyone was friendly and acting normal, she suspected it was only her conscience making her feel as though she wore a flashing neon sign announcing what she and Brett had been tempted to do.

"Mommy," Emily shouted above the roar of the surf. "Look at the castle we made!"

Joe Davenport, the off-duty fireman, grinned from ear-to-ear, obviously as proud of the creation as the kids were. And why shouldn't he be? It was an impressive structure, complete with dribbles of wet sand to decorate the towers on each corner.

"It's beautiful!" Caitlin shot her daughter a smile, then grabbed a towel and dried off.

"Did you enjoy your swim?" Kay asked. "I'm thinking about going in the water, too."

"It was nice," Caitlin said, keeping a more accurate description to herself. The swim had been incredible, sensual, hot. A mind-spinning assault on her sex drive—something she'd managed to keep in check with very little effort, until Brett moved in next door.

After she slipped on a pale pink sweatshirt and combed her wet hair, Brett introduced her to several guys he referred to as Logan's Heroes. And from his earlier disclosure, she realized they'd each been troubled teens who now lived life on the straight and narrow, thanks to Harry.

Dr. Luke Wynter, who'd arrived while Caitlin and Brett had taken their sensual dip in the water, had just gotten off duty at Oceana General.

"Fancy meeting you here," the sandy-haired E.R. resident said to her.

Caitlin knew the attractive young doctor, since they often worked together. "It's a small world."

Luke was a top-notch physician, with almost an obsessive dedication to his patients and the hospital. And it was nice to see him let down his guard among friends.

Had he actually been a delinquent at one time? His all-American good looks belied the fact. Stormy gray eyes didn't.

She wondered if she'd ever hear his story, learn how he'd met Harry.

Next, Brett introduced her to Hailey and Nick Granger.

"It's nice to meet you," Caitlin told the glowing, dark-haired woman who appeared to be about six months pregnant.

"Hailey is Harry's daughter," Brett explained.

Caitlin didn't see the resemblance to either Harry or Kay, although the young woman was attractive.

Brett placed a hand on Hailey's husband's shoulder. "And this is Nick."

"We've met," Caitlin said with a casual smile.

Just last week, Detective Granger had come to the hospital to investigate a brutal beating of an elderly man. The case had been turned over to homicide when it was determined that the retired banker was brain-dead.

The intense, dark-haired detective extended a hand. "It's nice to see you somewhere other than the trauma ward."

"You're right about that."

Nick had always reminded Caitlin of a tough, no-nonsense type on the job. But he'd certainly loosened up around Hailey and her family.

And he was especially attentive to his pregnant wife, something that was sweet and heartwarming to see.

As the evening progressed, Caitlin was glad she and Emily had come. She appreciated the welcome the Logans and their friends had offered her and the way they'd drawn her and Emily into the fold.

Every now and again, she stole a glance at Brett. And each time she did, he looked her way, too. It was as though he could sense her eyes on him, her interest, her curiosity.

Or was it more than that?

She wasn't sure what had happened to them out there, amidst the pounding surf, the setting sun, the shared passion. But there was no denying their friendship had taken a sexual turn.

Was that a bad thing?

Caitlin had been on her own for so darn long, and struggling to be strong, that she hadn't dated in years. Maybe her body was going through a natural rebellion against forced celibacy.

But that explanation didn't hold water.

She wasn't just craving sex. She was craving Brett and *his* hands, *his* lips. *His* body.

"Is anyone hungry?" Harry asked. "I'm ready to eat."

After a varied chorus of voices calling out, "I am," and "Me, too," Caitlin retrieved Emily from the sand castle and walked her to the bathroom, where an outdoor shower provided beachgoers a way to wash the sand away before going home.

As she maneuvered her daughter under the spray, she asked, "Are you having fun, honey?"

"Uh-huh. And when I grow up, I'm going to marry Bobby."

"You are?"

Emily nodded, eyes glimmering. "Even if he doesn't like Hello Kitty and thinks it's dumb."

Caitlin turned off the water and dried the child with one of the towels she'd packed. Then she dressed her in long pants and a Winnie-the-Pooh sweatshirt. "Okay, honey. Let's go eat."

When they returned to the fire, Brett was busy cooking hot dogs over the flame. He looked up and smiled. "How does she like hers fixed?"

"Just plain, the meat and the bun."

"And yours?" he asked.

She smiled. "I like the works."

He slid her a slow, crooked grin that suggested they weren't talking about hot dogs and all the trimmings. A sense of anticipation sent her pulse rate soaring.

An hour later, after everyone had eaten their fill and the sun had disappeared from sight, they sat around a crackling fire, chatting with each other or just enjoying the sound of the surf and the scent of wood smoke mingling with the ocean breeze.

Caitlin glanced at her daughter, who sat in Brett's lap with her head resting against his shoulder, her eyes closed in slumber.

Would Caitlin rest in his arms one day, too?

He tossed her a promising smile, one that allowed her dreams to take flight—the usual ones of family, love and all that was right in the world.

Whether either of them would admit it, they were becoming a family of sorts. At least, that's the way it felt to Caitlin.

Were Brett's thoughts going in that direction, too?

God help her, she hoped so. Because she'd love

to lean on him, to confide in him about the custody battle she was facing. To have him in her corner for the rest of her life.

Because, as much as she wanted to deny it, she was falling for the man. Deeply. Heart over head.

And she wondered whether he knew, whether he could sense it.

Brett glanced at the sweet pixie who'd plopped into his lap earlier, as though it was the most natural thing in the world for her to do.

For a man who didn't like being close to children, he was certainly getting used to the precious little girl in his arms, something that wasn't nearly as scary as it had once been.

Heck, even looking at Bobby, who was roasting marshmallows and making s'mores with his mom and dad, wasn't nearly as painful as it had been earlier. And he wasn't sure why.

Maybe because being around families like the Davenports and couples like the Logans and the Grangers made him believe that somehow, someway, someday, he and his son could be a family, too, even if it was only for one weekend a month.

Caitlin, he supposed, had something to do with the change in him. Her optimism. Her spirit. The way she made a single-parent home look inviting.

But it was more than a sense of family that drew him to her.

A whole lot more.

And being alone with her had done something to him, too. Something warm and mushy.

"Anyone else want another s'more?" Kristin asked, as she sandwiched a piece of chocolate and a melted marshmallow between two graham crackers.

"I do." Caitlin reached for the confection and broke it into two, the melted chocolate and marshmallow stretching into a gooey string. She lifted it to Brett's lips, feeding him.

As he munched on the standard bonfire delicacy, their eyes remained locked. And that sexual energy that had been bombarding them all night settled over them again.

Maybe he ought to reconsider his don't-get-involved-with-single-mothers philosophy—at least temporarily.

He reached for her hand, although he didn't have a clue why. Just wanted to, he supposed. And when he turned to look at her, he fell headfirst into her pretty smile.

What was the hold she had on him?

He shuffled the child in his arms, then gave Caitlin's hand a squeeze. "Should we take her home?"

"It's probably a good idea. It's past her bedtime."

He nodded, then graciously made their goodbyes, thanking the Logans for including them.

Caitlin offered her own gratitude and received a warm hug from Kay and another from Harry.

Then they headed for the parking lot, that sexual something surrounding them like an aura. When they reached the Explorer, Brett clicked the unlock button on the key chain, opened the rear passenger door and secured Emily in the seat.

"I really enjoyed meeting your friends," Caitlin said, as she climbed into the car. "They're nice people."

"Yeah. They're the best. I'm glad you got a chance to meet them."

They remained silent for the rest of the way home. Brett figured the memory of that hot kiss in the surf wasn't far from her thoughts, either.

He still wasn't sure about putting the moves on her. But if she offered him a kiss—or more than that—he wouldn't fight her on it.

As he pulled the Explorer into the complex and headed for the carport, he cleared his throat. "I'll carry Emily inside for you."

"Thanks, I'd appreciate it. In fact, I'll pour you a glass of wine, if you're up for it."

A neighborly offer?

Or a way to prolong their time together?

Either way, he wasn't ready to call it a night. "Sure, why not."

Minutes later, after they'd put Emily to bed, Caitlin went into the kitchen, and he followed her.

As she prepared to open a bottle of wine, he took the corkscrew from her hand. "I'll get it."

But as their fingers touched, stirring up that desire that had been brewing all evening, he didn't give a squat about the wine.

Nor did he want to wait for her to make the first move.

He might be sorry about this later, but he wasn't going to think about that now. All he wanted to do was taste her lips again, hold her close, press himself against her.

So he took her in his arms and lowered his mouth to hers.

Chapter Nine

Caitlin couldn't say that she hadn't expected the kiss, since she'd hoped her growing attraction to Brett wasn't one-sided.

But that didn't mean the heat of his touch, the intoxicating, chocolaty taste of his mouth, didn't take her by sweet surprise.

His musky cologne mingled with the faint smell of wood smoke and the salty ocean air that lingered in his T-shirt. And she inhaled slowly, just to savor his scent.

He pulled her close and ran a hand under the hem of her sweatshirt, skimming his fingers along her skin to the top of her swimsuit. As he reached under the material and caressed the swell of her breast, her nipples hardened and her breath caught.

She wanted to make love to him more than she'd ever thought possible. And for some reason, all her reservations about getting involved with him fell by the wayside.

Tired from her struggles to be strong and do the right thing, she leaned into his embrace, taking whatever he had to offer. She might not be able to depend on him to be at her side forever, but tonight, she needed him to love her. And she needed to feel him deep inside of her.

As he palmed her breast, his thumb caressed her nipple and sent her senses spinning. She was lost in a swirl of something that was far more powerful, more magical than a woman had a right to experience.

As the kiss deepened, he moaned into her mouth, pulling her flush against him. She realized he was feeling it, too. The desire to be one, to go all the way.

She broke the kiss, but only to whisper, "I'm not sure how I'll feel about this in the morning, but I want to make love tonight."

Brett couldn't have said it any better. He may have fought getting involved with her before, fought the desire that simmered in his blood, but she'd chased the fight out of him.

Passion clouded the air, making it hard to breathe, to think, to reason. Regret might be a climax away, but there wasn't a damn thing he wanted more than to bury himself deep within her—now.

Whatever she was doing to him, whatever she'd already done, scared him spitless, yet not enough to deny himself a night in her bed, a passion-filled night in her arms.

But reason came crashing to the forefront.

Sex with her had been on his mind, at least subliminally, since the first day he'd laid eyes on her, but he hadn't planned on that arousing swim in the ocean, hadn't planned on making love tonight.

"I want this, too," he told her. "But I don't have any…protection with me."

Although that didn't mean he couldn't make it good for her.

What kind of selfish bastard would leave her alone to cool off, while he jogged home and dug through the medicine cabinet and all the drawers to find a rubber that might not even be there?

"I might have a condom," she said, her breath coming out whisper soft against his shirt.

She might? Now that was the best news he'd heard all week. All year. His whole damn life.

She pulled away. "I haven't been involved with anyone in a long time, not since just after becoming Emily's mother."

Brett didn't usually give a damn about a woman's ex-lovers, but for some reason, he couldn't stifle his curiosity. Was the guy good to her? Had she loved him? What kind of a fool would let her go?

She offered him a wobbly smile, then took his hand and led him to her bedroom.

Checking out her decor was the last thing he intended to do, but he couldn't help but notice how her scent, her uniqueness, her femininity, practically permeated the pale green walls, the white frilly-style curtains.

She slipped inside her bathroom and dug through a drawer. When she pulled out a foil packet, she flashed him a rosy-cheeked grin that damn near sent his heart flying topsy-turvy.

Not his heart, he quickly corrected. His hormones.

He still feared the hold she had on him. But maybe making love would put things in perspective and help him get back on even ground.

As she studied the packet and twirled it in her hands, her brow furrowed. Then she brightened. "We're in luck. It doesn't expire for another couple of months."

He wanted to laugh out loud, to kiss the cute wrinkle in her brow. To relish the fact that she wanted this as badly as he did.

Instead, he took the condom and tossed it on the white goose-down comforter that covered her bed, then cupped her jaw with both hands. "Now, where were we?"

"Right here." She wrapped her arms around him, and he nuzzled the swanlike curve of her neck. She bent back her head, allowing him to press open-mouthed kisses along her throat.

He wanted to love her with a slow hand, to make things last all night long, but the fire in his blood burned out of control, leaving him with a desperate need only she could sate.

"Do you have any idea what you do to me?" he asked, his voice husky with desire.

"I think so." Her eyes lowered.

In shyness?

She lifted the hem of her sweatshirt over her head, revealing the black top of her bikini. Her slow but steady movements to take off her shirt mesmerized him.

After dropping it to the floor, she tugged at the black strings. Ever so slowly, she taunted him—although he suspected it wasn't on purpose—by peeling away the black satiny material of her swimsuit and unleashing two perfect breasts with taut dusky nipples hardened by her arousal.

Next came the shorts. As she slid the panty portion of her bikini over her hips and down her legs, he sucked in a breath, nearly choking on the honesty of his sentiment. "You're beautiful, Caitlin. And I feel as though I've been offered a special gift."

"Thank you. I feel that I've been given something, too."

Not of equal value, he realized. She deserved better than him. But he didn't let that stop him from shedding his shirt and slipping out of his trunks.

When they were both naked, he drew her into his arms. Her full breasts splayed against his chest, as their hands explored each other, caressing, taunting. But he couldn't get enough, not even when she melded against him.

For as long as he could, he fought the desire to lay her down, to make love to her like she wanted him to.

Like he wanted to.

But if he didn't plunge into her sweetness soon, he'd die from want of her.

He stepped toward the bed, taking her with him. And as they tumbled onto the comforter, he grappled for the condom. When he'd torn into the packet and protected them both, he gave her a lingering kiss that promised sexual pleasure yet to come. Then he loved her with his hands and his mouth until passion overcame them both.

As he hovered over her, she opened for him and placed her hands on his hips, as though guiding him home—where he belonged.

He entered her almost desperately, and she arched up to meet his thrusts, taking and giving until their passion peaked. He would have held back, prolonging the excitement, but he was lost in lust and passion, lost in her sweet embrace.

Their breathing, ragged and hot, played upon his senses, fanning his desire.

They balanced at the peak of a shaky precipice, barely hanging on.

"Let it go, honey," he whispered. "Don't hold back." Then he thrust deep.

Her breath caught, her fingernails clutched at his back and she cried out her pleasure as a powerful, breath-defying climax overtook them both, shoving them over the edge of control.

When the last orgasmic wave had passed, he didn't let go of her, didn't roll away. Didn't find an excuse to leave.

He couldn't seem to gather the energy.

Later—he had no idea how long—he lay in Caitlin's bed, with her head resting on his shoulder, his heart pounding from more than exertion. He knew he held more woman than he'd ever held before.

When he'd filled her womb to the hilt, he could feel his release to the depths of his heart.

To his heart?

Oh, no. Not that deep.

She'd merely touched his passion, his desire. His libido. It couldn't possibly be more than that. He might love the way it felt to thrust deep inside of her, love to hear her breathy whimpers, to see desire and fulfillment glaze her eyes as she climaxed in his arms.

But love *her?*

No way. He couldn't let that happen.

Brett couldn't give Caitlin or Emily what they deserved. How could he when he couldn't do the same for Justin?

As dawn crept through the slats of the miniblinds, Caitlin lay nestled in Brett's arms, amazed at the depth of her love for the man in her bed.

They shared a pillow now, but last night, they'd shared so much more. Hungry kisses. Breath-catching sexual peaks. Mind-spinning releases. But their joining had been more than just sex—so much more, that her heart had reached the bursting point.

Brett's slow and steady breathing lulled her, and the arm he'd draped around her breasts held her close.

She'd had reservations about getting involved with him at a time like this.

But not anymore. And she suspected he'd changed his mind, too. He sure hadn't made any excuses to leave her bed, other than to go into the bathroom and dig through the drawer to find another condom. As it was, they'd gone through three—all she'd been able to find when she'd hurriedly dug through the drawer.

As she savored the scent of their lovemaking, the warmth of his embrace, the intensity of all they'd experienced, she struggled with being a good hostess. For some reason, she thought about getting up and fixing a pot of coffee, something she always did immediately upon rising. And in the fridge, she had fresh orange juice. Maybe she ought to pour two glasses and bring them back to bed.

But she wasn't ready to leave the warmth and comfort of his arms, where the memory of their sweet, all-night sex marathon lingered. He'd been an incredible lover, making her think it was she who'd created the magic and set off fireworks during their lovemaking. And after a while, she nearly believed it.

She'd actually made noises and cried out while climaxing. Imagine that.

Of course, she was no expert when it came to sex. Before last night, she could count the number of times she'd made love on one hand, with fingers to spare.

Her only other experience had been nice, after that awkward first time. But it hadn't been anything like this. What a difference being in love made.

Last night, in Brett's capable arms, she'd learned

a lot of things about her body that she hadn't known before. And together, they'd touched the stars.

Brett nuzzled her head and placed a kiss on her temple, letting her know he was stirring.

"Good morning," she whispered. "Do you want me to put on some coffee and fix breakfast?"

He stroked the curve of her hip. "I don't eat in the morning. But coffee sounds good. Then I'd better cut out before Emily wakes up and finds me here."

"All right." As much as Caitlin hated to see him leave, she appreciated his thoughtfulness, since they were treading on uncharted ground, especially with the custody case hanging over her head.

Maybe, on Monday morning, she ought to call her attorney and get some advice about how to handle this change in her life. She didn't want a lover to jeopardize her position.

Or would it strengthen her case by offering a father figure to Emily?

As she climbed from bed, Brett ran a hand along her derriere. She glanced over her shoulder and flashed him a playful smile. "Don't tempt me, or we'll spend too much time in here and get caught."

"We're out of protection."

"Until I make a more thorough search of that drawer, or one of us goes to the pharmacy." She grabbed her robe from the closet. "If you'd like to take a shower, there are towels in the bathroom cupboard."

"I'll shower at home."

She nodded, then headed for the door. "The coffee will be ready in a couple of minutes."

"I'll meet you in the kitchen."

Moments later, they sat at the small breakfast table, listening to the coffee drip into the glass carafe.

"Any regrets?" he asked. "You thought there might be some in the morning."

"No. What about you?"

He shrugged. "I don't know. I guess it depends."

"On what?"

"On where we go from here." He placed his forearms on the table, his hands half-clasped in front of him.

Where did *he* want things to go? His expression was difficult to read.

"Last night made things a bit complicated," she admitted.

"I know."

Did he? Had Gerald or Mary told him about Zack, about the custody fight?

She wasn't sure, but she decided it was best to lay her cards on the table. "I'd like to talk to my attorney before we get any more involved."

"Your attorney?" He pulled his hands from the table and straightened, his eyes widening as though she'd snuck up on him and jabbed him with a syringe. "What do you mean?"

"Emily's father wants custody of her, and he's taking me to court."

With his brow furrowed, his mouth tensed, he leaned back in his chair, pulling away. Distancing himself? "You've got to be kidding."

"I wish I were." She got up from her seat and

poured them each a cup of coffee. She handed him one, then sweetened hers with a spoonful of sugar and added a bit of milk.

He gripped his cup with both hands, but didn't take a drink. "The guy has been missing in action for four years. Why does he want custody now?"

"He's been in prison, but he's going to be paroled soon."

"Her father's in prison?" The tension in his face suggested she should have explained some of this to him earlier, even though neither of them had expected to become intimate. "What did he do?"

"He was arrested for his involvement in an armed robbery at a convenience store. One of his friends, Ray Montalvo, shot the owner in the back, leaving the man paralyzed. And Zack, Emily's dad, testified against Ray and received a plea bargain."

"Are you talking about Zack Henderson?"

"Yes." She took a sip of coffee, trying to savor the familiar morning taste, needing a jolt of caffeine, but getting little satisfaction. "Do you know him?"

"Not personally. But I remember hearing about the case. Harry had tried to reach out to him before he was arrested, but obviously those efforts failed."

She didn't doubt the Bayside criminal justice system had incarcerated more than a few delinquents who'd turned a deaf ear to Harry and fell through the treacherous cracks. And Zack was obviously one of them.

Brett still held his cup below mouth level. "Maybe

Harry could talk to Zack and get him to agree to liberal visitation, instead of custody."

"No." Caitlin stiffened, her heart pounding out an objection that throbbed in her ears. "I'm not going to give up my daughter, not even for an occasional visit with that man. Zack is a convicted felon, a criminal. And I'll fight him with everything I've got, every penny, every breath."

"I can understand how you feel, Caitlin, but the man is still her father. For Emily's sake, you need to try and work out something amiable. Shared custody, maybe."

"No." She rubbed her hands along her arms, wondering when the chill in the room had kicked up.

He reached across the table and took her hand, his thumb slowly stroking her skin. "Caitlin, I realize you're in a precarious situation. But I don't think going to court is the right way to handle this."

She opened her mouth to object, to cry out a list of reasons why Zack Henderson should never be involved in Emily's life. But she held her tongue. What was there to say? Brett had told her about his early years, about the custody battles his parents had waged. It was clear he wouldn't support her in this fight. And the discussion was over, as far as she was concerned.

She and Brett may have had something special last night, but whatever it was had faded with the dawn. With reality.

Brett's lack of support and understanding disappointed her, of course. But he hadn't really let her down. After all, she'd never had anyone in her corner before, never had anyone she could depend upon, other than the Blackstones and the attorney she'd retained.

So what if Brett wasn't up for the fight?

That was okay. She'd just have to battle the system alone. But wasn't that what she'd expected to do all along?

To go it alone?

She'd faced pain and heartbreak before. And this was no different. She was a survivor—strong and self-reliant.

But this time around, she was facing the biggest battle of her life. And her vulnerability was more than unsettling.

It scared her to death.

But she wouldn't back down, wouldn't compromise. Not when Emily's life and welfare hung in the balance. And apparently, that was something the man she'd come to love would never understand.

Brett gave Caitlin's hand a gentle squeeze, but her fingers remained stiff, unresponsive.

He knew she was in a tough position, and he wanted to support her. "I don't want to see Emily uprooted from the only home she's ever had. Nor do I like the idea of an ex-con taking part in her upbringing."

Caitlin, her eyes fixed on the table, fingered the handle on her coffee cup. "I understand."

Did she?

Hell, he still wasn't sure if he did. All he knew was

that he couldn't allow himself to get sucked into a mess—financially or otherwise—that would only bring misery to the child he'd grown to care about, not to mention stir up memories he'd like to forget.

Besides, his presence in the courtroom would serve no purpose. Hadn't his parents' situation blown sky-high when his mom brought a stepfather on the scene? What would a boyfriend do to the mix?

"I wish I could support you in this, but I don't believe adults should fight over their kids. I'm a father who hasn't seen his son in five years. And I know there are a lot of reasons why a man might stay out of touch and change his mind later." He gave her hand another gentle squeeze, and when she lifted her eyes and caught his gaze, he opened up, sharing his heart, his pain, his sacrifice. "My son's name is Justin, and I'd do anything for him. I think about him every day of my life, not just when the monthly child support allotment comes out of my paycheck."

"Why don't you see him?" she asked.

For a ton of reasons. His job with the Navy, for one. The fact the kid didn't even know him for another. And because Brett couldn't offer the boy the things David and Kelly could offer him. And to be honest, deep down, he was afraid his own unstable childhood had left him lacking in the family and daddy department.

"I'm not happy about the situation," Brett clarified. "But he was just a baby when his mother and I split up, and I was on active duty. I couldn't very well share custody with his mother."

"What about when he was older?" she asked.

"I saw him from time to time, as often as my deployments would allow. But when he was about two, Kelly—his mom and my ex—started giving me a hard time whenever I asked to come and visit. She said my presence was confusing him."

"Was it?"

He shrugged. "Justin seemed shy and distant when I came around. I don't know much about kids, but maybe my visits were stressing him out." He took a deep breath and blew it out. "And to be honest, it was stressing me out, too. Justin was only two, but he'd already started calling her husband Daddy."

"So you stopped visiting?"

"I did what I thought was best for my son."

"Maybe things have changed. Maybe she'd be more agreeable to you visiting now."

He hoped so, but he doubted it. When Justin was four, he'd tried again. He'd called Kelly and asked to take Justin for a weekend, and she'd flipped out and started bawling. Then she'd threatened to fight him, just like Caitlin had said she'd do if Zack Henderson wanted to be a part of Emily's life.

Are you out of your mind? Kelly had shrieked. *You can't come waltzing into our lives like this. He doesn't even know you.*

But he's my son, Brett had countered. *And I was given the right to reasonable visitation.*

I'm not going to agree to that now. I can't. I won't.

When he tried to remind her that Justin was his

son, she'd cursed a blue streak, told him to talk to her lawyer, then slammed down the phone.

The mention of courts and attorneys turned his gut inside out, and he'd decided to stay away. To give Justin time to grow up.

"She sounds unfair, if not unstable."

"Only when it comes to talking and compromising with me. So I've stayed out of Justin's life, rather than put him through the fights and the legal hell I went through as a kid."

"This is different." Caitlin pulled her hand from his, severing their connection. Then she crossed her arms and sat back in her chair. "I'm not fighting to protect my selfish interests, like your parents did or like your ex-wife is doing. I'm fighting for Emily."

"I know it's different. But it's the fighting, the court crap. The arguments."

"You didn't have to worry about your son's safety and well-being when you chose to let his mother raise him alone."

"You're right. His mother and I may have had more than our fair share of differences and heated arguments, but I never had to worry about Justin being cared for." He took a deep breath, trying to gather his thoughts, to explain his position. "But I still believe adults need to compromise when it comes to sharing their children."

"You're asking me to find some kind of middle ground with a convicted felon, a guy who robbed a convenience store, a guy whose friend shot a man in the back. A criminal who shouldn't be trusted to be alone with Emily, let alone be allowed to raise her in his household."

A toilet flushed, alerting them that they were no longer alone in the house.

"We can talk about this later," Brett said. "I'd like to leave before she finds us together. I don't want her getting the idea that I spent the night."

"That's probably for the best." Caitlin stood and walked him to the door.

He bent to kiss her, and she offered her cheek.

Whatever intimacy they'd shared last night was over. And he ought to be glad. This was just the kind of thing he'd always tried to avoid.

"I'll talk to you later," he said.

She nodded, then closed the door and let him walk out of her home, out of her life.

He ought to run like hell, to thank his lucky stars that he'd gotten out of there by the skin of his teeth.

But for some damn reason, he felt more trapped than ever.

Chapter Ten

One more time in Caitlin's arms, one more night in her bed, and Brett would be toast.

What had gotten into him?

Not only had he made love with a single mom, a woman who was fighting for custody of her child, but he'd spent the entire night with her. Why hadn't he slipped away after the first time they'd made love?

He stood under the hot, pulsating shower, letting the water pound into him. But he didn't feel a damn bit refreshed. Or relieved that he'd escaped.

Instead, he felt like a jerk for the way things had ended this morning—and for more reasons than that.

First of all, there was the sex, which had been incredible—the best he'd ever had, actually. But it complicated things big time.

As the steam filled the shower stall, his mental vision seemed to clear. And as much as he hated to admit it, hated to contemplate the ramifications, he'd enjoyed sleeping with Caitlin and waking in her arms. And now, after the loving and the intimacy they'd shared, he regretted getting in so deep, especially because of the pending court case.

But it was more than a reminder of the crap he'd dealt with as a child and his determination to stay out of a similar situation that bothered him. It was the damn fear he didn't like admitting to—his fear of facing Kelly, of asking to see his son and having her threaten to take him to court.

Yet there was an even bigger fear. What if Kelly actually agreed to regular visitation, and Brett bombed at being a father?

Of course, he hadn't wanted Caitlin to know that. So he'd used the excuse of Emily finding them together to hurry home, to bail out of the emotional quagmire he'd gotten into.

And that's just what this whole damn mess felt like—a swampy bog of quicksand that threatened to pull him under.

He grabbed the towel from the rack and dried off, then slipped on a pair of jeans and a shirt. He'd used deodorant out of habit, but since he didn't feel like being more than a hermit today, he didn't bother shaving.

Maybe he ought to hole up with the cats, find a

ballgame on TV. Or better yet, he ought to take a nap, since he hadn't gotten much sleep last night, not after sleeping with Caitlin, who'd been able to turn him inside out with only a smile, a skim of her fingers, a catch of her breath.

Oh, for cripes sake. Get over it, Tanner.

A meow wound through the doorway of the bedroom, where Fred had just parked his furry butt. He meowed again, as though trying to say something in cat-language.

"What's the matter, buddy?"

The cat merely looked at him with an ain't-life-the-pits expression.

"Did those kittens annoy you again?" Brett scooped the cat into his arms and carried him to the living room, where Fluffy chased Princess to the top of the carpet-covered tower. He stroked Fred's head, taking time to fondle his ear—something he'd realized the cat really liked. "Why don't you and I go have a cup of coffee. I've got a lot of stuff to work through."

Once in the kitchen, he set Fred on the tile floor and gave him a kitty treat before measuring out coffee grounds and brewing a pot that didn't taste anywhere near as good as Caitlin's had.

Damn. He had to break free of that death grip she had on him before it was too late.

Of course, that didn't mean he didn't care about her or about what she was going through. Nor did it mean he liked the idea of an ex-con coming into contact with Emily. Zack could very well be using his parenthood as a ploy to convince the parole board he planned to become an upstanding citizen.

But Brett got a knot in his gut when he thought of a guy just wanting to see his kid. Especially since, in this case, he found himself identifying—at least a little—with Zack.

Maybe it was the fact that he and Zack had so much in common. They'd both been kids who'd rebelled as a means to deal with a crappy childhood. Hell, if Harry hadn't stepped in, Brett might have ended up in jail, too. So maybe that's why he had a hard time seeing Zack as just some big bad criminal.

Guys made mistakes.

Besides, Brett couldn't blame the man for wanting to be a part of Emily's life—if Zack was sincere.

And Brett sure as heck didn't need a degree in psychology to know why he felt that way.

How would Kelly react if he asked to exercise his parental rights?

Flip out again and threaten to call an attorney, he supposed, just like she'd done the last time he'd tried to talk to her.

And just like Caitlin was doing now.

Why couldn't parents put a kid's best interest first?

Of course, in Caitlin's case, he had to give her credit for having a legitimate reason for not wanting Zack Henderson to be a part of Emily's life.

But Zack had paid his debt to society. What if he really wanted to start fresh and be a father to his daughter?

Brett wasn't sure if there was anything he could

do to help, unless it was learning what kind of man Zack had become.

And who better to ask than Harry?

He poured a cup of coffee, then picked up the phone and dialed the number he knew by heart.

The retired detective answered on the fourth ring.

"Hello, Harry. It's Brett. I just wanted to thank you again for including us last night. We had a great time."

"I'm glad you could make it."

Brett paused for a moment, trying to segue into his question, but figured it was best just to blurt it out. "Hey, do you remember a guy named Zack Henderson?"

"Yeah. He's at Riverview Correctional Facility, wrapping up a five-year sentence."

"What do you know about him?"

"Before his arrest, I saw potential in him and tried to help. And for a while, I thought I'd reached him. He'd agreed to attend a barbecue down at the Bay-side Marina one Saturday night about five years ago, but he failed to show up. I learned later that he and Ray Montalvo had been involved in an armed rob-bery at a convenience store."

"What part did Zack play?"

"He swore up and down he was innocent, that he'd been in the wrong place at the wrong time. It was a classic defense and tough for a jury to accept. He and Montalvo had once been pretty tight."

"Did you buy Zack's story?"

"I'd really like to believe him. But Zack, by his own admission, had ridden in Montalvo's car and was inside the convenience store when the robbery went down. They had him on tape, too."

"So what do you think five years in prison have done to him?"

When Harry didn't respond right away, Brett envisioned him running a hand along his receding hairline, a habit the older man favored when he contemplated something. "I haven't seen Zack in nearly five years, but from what I heard from a buddy who works at the prison, he's kept his nose clean. His uncle's neighbor owns a construction company, and Zack plans to work for him."

"Do you know anything about Zack having a daughter?"

"I knew he'd been dating a girl who'd gotten pregnant just before the robbery. He seemed concerned about how she'd get along with him behind bars, but I have to admit, I lost contact with him after that. I really don't know how things panned out."

Brett didn't know how much of Caitlin's plight to share with Harry. But he figured it wouldn't hurt to have the retired detective in their corner.

Their corner? Oh for cripes sake. Talking to Harry about Emily's father was about as involved as Brett wanted to get in this mess.

But he still had a few questions that needed answers. "From what I understand, the young woman was fatally shot in a drive-by shooting, and her baby was delivered by an emergency caesarian."

"Hmmm. I wonder if that was Teresa Carmichael."

"Who?"

"A young woman who'd become involved in the homeless shelter that Kay's church supports. She was pregnant and waiting at a bus stop when the same thing happened to her."

"That could be the same woman. But either way, Zack's daughter is the little girl you met at the beach."

"No kidding? She's a beautiful child."

"Caitlin has been Emily's foster mother since birth." Brett fiddled with the telephone cord. "She loves that little girl and wants to adopt her, but Zack won't allow it."

"That's a tough situation for everyone involved, especially Emily."

"Yeah, my sentiments exactly. You know how I feel about adults fighting over kids."

"Yes, I do. And that reminds me. Have you seen Justin?"

Now Brett was the one running a hand over his forehead. "Not yet. After the last time I talked to Kelly, and now seeing how Caitlin is reacting to Zack, I'm not sure how to broach the subject again."

Or whether he should talk to Kelly at all.

"That's not the same thing," Harry said. "You're Justin's father and have been supporting him financially for years. You also have court-ordered visitation."

"Yeah. I know. Caitlin pointed out the same thing." But Brett had a feeling she'd fight Zack for custody, even if he'd been at a seminary and studying for the ministry these past four or five years.

"Legally," Harry said, "Kelly can't keep you from Justin."

"I know that. But I don't want to have to go through the courts."

Neither did he want to spend the rest of his life not knowing his son. It was a real catch-22.

Harry didn't respond, so Brett added, "Maybe I'll call Kelly in the next day or so."

At least, that's what he'd been telling himself ever since coming back to Bayside after his last tour of duty.

"I think that would be a good idea."

"Yeah, well, I'd better go, Harry. I've got to feed the cats." He used it as an excuse, even though Greg had one of those big canisters that kept the food coming each time the cats ate a couple of morsels.

After the line disconnected, Brett struggled with his options—at least as far as Caitlin went.

He wanted to do what was best for Emily. And without a doubt, she'd be better off with Caitlin as her mother. But her father had rights, too, and a compromise was the only way to go.

But Brett feared that Caitlin wasn't going to budge, even if Zack agreed to an occasional weekend visitation. Not without a court order.

He had no idea what a court battle would do to Emily—not to mention what it would do to Caitlin, if she was ordered to give up her daughter.

And he'd be damned if he wanted to see Caitlin hurt. His pretty neighbor tugged at the heartstrings he'd thought had been knotted up for good.

Hey, how about that? For a guy who'd managed to avoid emotional entanglements in the past, he'd certainly gotten caught in a doozy.

Should he get out of the way?

Or back up Caitlin, going as far as sitting with her in court and offering her the money she needed for what might prove to be a long, expensive battle?

The answer should have been clear.

But it wasn't.

By early afternoon, Brett had developed a severe case of cabin fever. His great escape had only boxed him in.

For some damn reason, he was compelled to talk to Caitlin, although he wasn't exactly sure about what.

Their relationship, or whatever it was, he supposed.

And her situation with Emily.

As a furry scuffle broke out by the bookshelf, he turned to the orange tabby—wasn't that the one named Princess?—peering out between the bushy leaves of a rhododendron like a lion in the jungle.

Crazy little cat.

She was hiding like some sly, tough guy.

Like Brett was, he realized, holed up in this damned condo.

Ah, hell. Enough of this crap.

He placed the television remote on the coffee table, next to a half-empty can of soda, then strode outside to go find Caitlin. It was time to talk.

The truth was, he didn't like the way things had

ended between them. And the sooner he faced her, the better.

But as he got halfway across the lawn that stretched between their condos, he saw her step out of the Blackstone's place and close the door. She was dressed in hospital garb and wearing white nurse's shoes, so it was obvious she was heading off to work.

On Saturday?

He knew nurses didn't have bankers' hours, but she hadn't said anything to him about working today. But then, why would she? It's not as though they'd talked about the future.

"Do you have a minute?" he asked.

Her steps slowed, and she shot him a surprised look. Her lips parted, then she glanced at her watch. "Just a few. I'm going to the hospital to cover for a co-worker who's sick."

"I don't like the way things ended between us yesterday."

"Neither do I. But it's okay. With the custody hearing coming up, I don't think me having a relationship with you is in Emily's best interests."

"You're probably right. And I'm not sure a relationship is in *your* best interests, either. I can be deployed at any time, and that doesn't make for a very stable romance."

"I understand." She tucked a strand of hair behind her ear and offered him an emotion-laden smile that was impossible to decipher. But rather than shrug it off, as he was accustomed to doing, he longed to know exactly what she was thinking, feeling. And that made no sense at all. Not if he was going to get out in one piece.

"Don't worry about what happened last night," she said. "It was just one of those things."

Normally, he'd be the first to admit she was right. Sex was a healthy outlet, and one that didn't need any emotional ties or encumbrances. And with her having that kind of attitude, he had an easy out.

But there was nothing easy about this damned relationship they'd tumbled into. Hell, the whole mess scared him senseless.

Maybe because the sex had been so damn good.

That had to be it.

"We satisfied our sexual curiosity," she added. "There's no harm in that."

"It was more than sex," he said, immediately wanting to suck the words back in his mouth. What the hell was he admitting?

She smiled, her cheeks taking on a pink tinge. "I'm glad you feel that way."

What way?

He sure as hell didn't know what was brewing in the far regions of his heart. Nor did he even want to think about it.

"So you're okay with letting last night slip into memory mode?" he asked.

She nodded. "At this point, I'm not sure what else to do with it. If you were able to support my efforts to fight for Emily, we could have seen what developed. But I need more than a couple of earth-spinning climaxes right now."

He'd known it had been good for her. For him, too. But hearing her put it into words made his pride puff up like a Christmas goose. Of course, he'd be wise to remember the fate of plump fowl in December.

Or had his goose been cooked already?

In his defense, he added, "I don't want to see either of you hurt. Not you, and certainly not Emily."

She nodded, but he still didn't think she understood where he was coming from. Where Emily's father might be coming from.

"Maybe you should meet with Zack, rather than allow your attorneys to do the talking."

She scrunched her brow, and her eyes narrowed. "You want me to go to the prison and visit a man I don't even know?"

He wasn't sure exactly what he was suggesting. "I think, when it comes to kids, parents ought to be able to compromise."

"In most cases, that's probably true," she said. "But I'm sure Phyllis McAree, my attorney, would advise against it."

"I wouldn't doubt that. It would be in her financial interests if this case blew sky-high."

"Think what you want, but Phyllis has been upfront with me since day one, and I'm going to take her advice."

Brett knew he was barking up an empty tree. But he couldn't help offering one more thing for her to think about. "When I was a kid, the judge sent my parents and me to family mediation. And the counselor told my mom and dad the story about King

Solomon and the two women who fought over a baby, each claiming to be the mother."

"I'm familiar with the story. Solomon told the women he would cut the child in half so they could share."

"And then one woman cried out that she'd lied, that the other woman should take the baby. Solomon determined that the one willing to give up the child, rather than see it harmed, was the real mother."

Caitlin crossed her arms, standing her ground, unbending, unyielding. "Zack should be the one to walk away from Emily. I can't."

"Not without a fight," he supplied.

No, Caitlin acknowledged silently. Not without a fight.

She glanced at her wristwatch again, realizing she didn't have time to continue this conversation much longer. She had to be at the hospital soon. And besides that, she'd grown tired of arguing and trying to explain why Zack shouldn't be a part of Emily's life.

Just the thought of losing her daughter clawed at her chest. She looked heavenward, as tears welled in her eyes, as emotion clogged her heart, her throat, her mouth.

The dark secret she'd fought hard not to share, not to reveal to anyone, crashed to the forefront. But Brett wasn't the only one with a past that dictated how he viewed his future. His memories influenced all his decisions, his belief system. And in spite of feeling as though sharing her past was a waste of breath, she decided to open up, unsure of how much of the nightmare would come tumbling out.

She took a slow, steady breath, then released it. "My mom was an on-again off-again druggie, and I spent my early years in and out of homeless shelters."

"I'm sorry," he said, the soft tone of his voice laced with compassion. Honesty.

She nodded an acknowledgement, a silent thanks-for-your-concern, then bit her bottom lip, almost afraid to go on, although she wasn't sure why.

Embarrassment? Shame? Realization that no matter what she said, her words would be useless when it came to swaying a man who'd allowed his own painful past to dictate his sense of right and wrong?

She continued anyway. "When I was twelve, my mom was arrested, and the court finally stepped in and placed me in a stable home." She thought about the Reillys', the love and acceptance she'd found.

For the first time in her life, she'd had a bedroom of her own and three square meals a day. And she had a sister and a brother she could almost claim as family.

She glanced up, saw him trying to deal with what she'd revealed. Or maybe he was just trying to come up with an acceptable response. "Being taken from my mother was a good thing. *Really.*"

Was that skepticism she read in his eyes or sympathy. She supposed it didn't matter.

"I no longer had to stand with her on street corners with a hand-scrawled cardboard sign and beg for money. And I didn't have to worry where I'd sleep each night. In foster care, I was able to get a taste of what a real family was like."

"And that's why you wanted to provide Emily with something similar," he said.

She could have let it end with that, but she went on with her story—maybe because she needed to hear herself say it out loud. "The court ordered my mother to a state-funded rehab."

"Did it help?"

She clicked her tongue. "I guess you could say that. She came out sober. But the problem was, she wanted me back."

This time, he didn't question her. He just let her talk.

"I suppose, in our own dysfunctional way, we loved each other. But I'd gotten tired of living with her addiction and with her lousy choice of friends and lovers. So, even at thirteen, I knew better than to expect miracles from her stint in rehab." An unexpected tear slipped down her cheek, and she swiped at it with the back of a hand. "I didn't want to leave the family I was with and go back to live with her, so I begged my foster parents and caseworker not to let me go. But no one cared enough to fight for me."

He shoved his hands in his pockets, as though refusing to reach out, to touch her, to offer a hug. And that was just as well. She didn't think his embrace would help. Not when the worst of her revelation was yet to come.

"To make a fresh start, my mother decided to relocate in San Diego. And about two months later, her new boyfriend, some guy she'd met at the pool hall where she worked as a waitress, came home drunk and cussing up a storm about her messing around with one of his friends. And things escalated from there." She sought his gaze, trying to gauge whether he could handle the rest without thinking of her as a freak, a victim, which is how she'd seen herself during those awkward teen years, when the case was still fresh. When it seemed that everyone in school was pointing and whispering about her.

Something had settled in his eyes, although she wasn't sure what. Sympathy maybe. Understanding?

"I watched from the hall as he began to beat her, first with his fists, then with a bulky glass ashtray he grabbed from the lamp table. Seeing the blood, hearing her screams, scared me to death, but I gathered my senses, ran to my bedroom, climbed out the window and ran down the street calling for help. But it was too late. When the police arrived, my mother was dead."

Brett took her in his arms, holding her close, whispering to soothe her. "Oh, God, honey. I'm so sorry. A child shouldn't have to witness something like that."

Her sentiments exactly, which was why she wanted to protect Emily from a similar fate. But she accepted Brett's comfort, savoring the warmth of his embrace, yet wise enough to know she'd temporarily touched a soft spot in his heart.

This embrace wasn't the same as meeting on a level playing field and having him tell her he loved her, that he'd support her in her struggles to not only gain custody of Emily, but to adopt her.

He whispered another, "I'm sorry."

His sympathy helped, she supposed. But she didn't have time to linger in his arms, not when his compassion didn't come with his full support.

Or better yet, with a confession of love.

So she drew back and wiped her eyes with her fingers. "So you'll have to forgive me for not seeing things your way, for not wanting to recognize the biological contribution to a child's life."

He started to object, but she didn't stop long enough to listen.

"I've got to go. I'm late to work."

"Maybe we can talk later," he said to her back.

"Yeah, maybe." But she was finished talking, opening up and sharing her pain.

As she unlocked the driver's door and began to climb into her car, she glanced over her shoulder one last time.

He just stood there, watching. Silence masked his thoughts and feelings.

So she slid into the driver's seat, closed the door and drove away. But no matter how far she drove, she couldn't escape the pain, the memories or the fear.

Brett just didn't get it.

He couldn't comprehend her determination to fight for her daughter. But that didn't matter.

Every child deserved to have one person in the world who was willing to fight for her.

Chapter Eleven

Brett stood on the lawn near the carport and watched as Caitlin drove away. He'd never been able to deal very well with emotional garbage, with knowing what to say, what to do. And this time he'd really been stumped.

The story she'd told him had turned his heart inside out. He hurt for the child she'd once been, for what she'd been through. And he understood why she intended to fight for Emily's best interests.

Still, he wished she'd try negotiation as the first step, even though it didn't appear as though she'd even consider a compromise.

In that respect, she wasn't so different from his ex, which is probably why his thoughts drifted to Kelly.

She'd had a similar attitude, when he'd asked to start seeing Justin on a regular basis.

Was it a mom thing? The same biological process that made a mother bear desperate to protect her cub?

Or was it merely human nature?

He tried to see Caitlin's side, to think about the loss she would suffer if forced to give up Emily. And in spite of his belief that adults shouldn't drag their kids to court, he had to admit she had a point.

Zack Henderson might be using his parenthood to convince the parole board he was ready to become a decent law-abiding member of the community.

If so, then what?

Emily's fate would be determined by a judge.

Damn it. *That's* why he had never wanted to get involved with a single mom in the first place. It was too much of a reminder of what he'd lived with day after day.

Or rather, what he lived without.

Brett swore under his breath. How could he even consider supporting Caitlin in a fight for her child, when he wasn't willing to fight for his own son?

He'd been a fool to let things get out of hand with Caitlin. The relationship had been doomed from the start. And he was even more foolish to stand out here in the middle of the complex, like some poor bastard whose woman had just driven off into the sunset with another guy.

Scoffing at himself for letting his emotions get the better of him, he headed back to the house—although there wasn't any reason to hole up there.

Maybe he ought to head for the beach. Try to get some fresh air and sunshine. Try to clear his head.

That's what he'd do.

But an hour later, as the gulls cried in the distance, as the salty breeze filled his lungs, as the waves crashed upon the shore, he didn't feel one bit better about the mess he'd allowed himself to fall into.

And it wasn't merely because of Caitlin.

If he wanted to show her the value of working out an amicable agreement with Emily's father, he had to pull off a compromise of his own.

The time had come to confront Kelly with what was fair, with what was right—in spite of how daunting the visit seemed.

Brett wasn't sure how long he'd parked in front of the house on Periwinkle Lane. Long enough to bolster his courage, he supposed.

He studied the white stucco walls, the pale teal trim, the freshly mowed lawn, the colorful birdhouse flag that hung over the porch.

There'd been a white Chevy pick-up parked here before. David's vehicle, he'd assumed.

Today, only the blue minivan rested in the drive. Was Kelly the only one home? If so, that would be best, wouldn't it? Or would David's presence help to keep her calm, reasonable?

Oh, what the hell. It was now or never.

He climbed from the Explorer and cut across the street, then he strode up the walkway that was flanked by colorful flower beds.

The last time he'd talked to Kelly about wanting to spend more time with Justin, it had been over the telephone. Had that been a mistake? Would it have been better to talk face-to-face?

He stood before the floral welcome mat, wondering what kind of reception he'd get.

It didn't matter, he supposed. He couldn't handle being out of Justin's life any longer. And he wanted a relationship with his son, even if he was referred to as Uncle Brett.

He lifted a hand to knock, then decided to ring the bell instead. After doing so, he shoved his hands in his pockets and waited for Kelly to answer.

Instead, a small, dark-haired boy with big blue eyes swung open the door.

Justin.

His son.

When he'd been younger, his hair had been lighter. A golden-blond. And he hadn't had freckles across his nose back then, had he?

Brett cleared his throat, hoping to dislodge the words. "Is your mom home?"

The boy nodded, then called his mother to the door.

"Yes," Kelly said, as she dried her hands on the edge of the apron she wore and entered the living room. Her eyes lit on Brett, and recognition registered on her face.

She'd gained a little weight, although he thought it looked good on her, making her appear more maternal, more genuine. More down to earth. Did that mean she would be willing to hear him out?

He offered a smile, hoping she realized he hadn't introduced himself to the boy. He knew better than to come waltzing up to the door and stir things up without any thought to the consequences.

She placed a hand on Justin's shoulder, in a protective way, as though she wanted to hold on to him, to keep him from bolting out the door with his father. "This is a surprise."

"I figured it would be. But I'd like to talk to you, if that's okay." He glanced at the boy, felt his heart thud in his chest. "In private."

"Of course."

Was it his imagination? Or had a flood of relief washed over her, too?

"Justin, why don't you go over to Scotty's house. Ask his mother if it's all right if you play for about thirty minutes."

"Okay." The boy didn't move right away. He stood in the doorway, looking at Brett.

Was he remembering the last time Brett had come to visit? Did he have any idea how the two of them were related?

He supposed those were questions he'd have to ask Kelly, assuming their conversation could remain civil.

She nudged Justin's shoulder. "Be sure to mind your manners at Scotty's house. And watch for cars when you cross the street."

"Uh-huh." Justin flashed a lopsided grin, then dashed out the door.

"Come on inside," she said, leading Brett to the living room.

He wiped his feet on the mat, just in case his shoes were dirty. Kelly had always been fussy about things like that. In the past, he hadn't cared about tracking dirt in the house. But he suspected that was because he'd liked being rebellious, a thorn in her persnickety backside.

Things were different now.

She took a seat on an overstuffed chair that had been upholstered in a striped material that matched the floral print of the sofa, on which he sat.

"It's been killing me not to see Justin," he admitted. "And I don't want to create problems for your family. But I want a relationship with him."

She sat back in the chair, her hands resting on the armrests. "I was afraid this day would come."

"I don't want to confuse him, but he's my son, Kelly."

"I know that."

"And I'm not asking you to disrupt your lives. I'm willing to compromise. I just want to get to know him, to see him, even if it's only once in a while." He raked a hand through his hair, realizing he'd need to get it cut someday soon. "It's not as though I've been a deadbeat dad. At least, financially."

"You've been more than fair about that."

"So how do we progress from here?" he asked, afraid she'd make references to her attorney, and if she did, not at all sure how he'd respond.

"I don't know." She blew out a ragged sigh. "I realize it was wrong of me, but I never told him about you. He thinks David is his father."

A sharp lance cut across his chest, but rather than cry out or complain, he nodded. "When I saw him last, he was calling your husband Daddy. I guess that's only normal, since David has raised him, and I haven't been around."

Her teeth bit into her bottom lip, and she twirled a strand of her hair, a nervous habit she'd always had. "David and I wanted to have another baby, but we weren't able to conceive. I don't want to go into the particulars, but Justin is the only child we'll be able to have."

Brett wanted to lash out, to tell her he hadn't wanted to be out of the picture, but that it had been her attitude and her threats to take him to court that had kept him away. But that would only create animosity, something that wouldn't help the compromise he so desperately wanted.

And blaming it all on Kelly wasn't fair either.

He'd been afraid of being a father, afraid that his dysfunctional upbringing would cause him to somehow fail his son.

But wasn't it enough to admit that fact to himself? Did he have to make a confession like that to Kelly?

Besides, maybe he wouldn't be a failure in the daddy department. Hadn't Emily grown attached to him?

Like he'd become attached to her?

And her mother?

Kelly clasped her hands in her lap, her fingers fidgeting with each other. "I'm sorry for my outburst the last time we talked, but David was having some serious medical problems at the time, and I was afraid I was losing him. The fear of losing Justin to you was too much for me to contemplate then."

"I hope David is doing better," Brett said. And he meant it. The guy had apparently taken good care of Kelly and Justin.

"He's much better." She nibbled at her lip again and studied her hands, then caught his gaze. "The cancer appears to be in remission now."

"That's good."

She nodded. "Yes, it is."

He didn't speak, didn't press. Hopefully, the fact they were talking and not making threats or angry retorts was a good thing.

"You have a right to spend time with Justin," she said. "And to be involved in his life. But to tell you the truth, I'm not sure how to go about straightening things out now."

"I understand. But I want you to know something. I wouldn't hurt Justin for the world. And I don't want to come between him and the man he thinks is his father. I appreciate all David has done for him."

"He's been a loving father," she admitted. "And this is going to be tough on him."

"It's been tough on me, too."

She rubbed her palms against the armrests, another nervous gesture, he realized.

"Can you give me some time to work this through?" she asked. "David and I will need to talk it over. And we'll have to decide the best way to tell him."

Brett had asked for a compromise, and he'd been given one. "Yeah. I'll give you some time."

The front door swung open, and Justin entered the room. "Scotty got in trouble for breaking a window in his family room. And his mom won't let him play for two whole hours."

"How did he break the window?" Kelly asked.

"He was chasing his big sister through the house with the broom, and he got the window instead." Justin turned and studied Brett. "Hi."

Brett reached out a hand, not sure if that was the right way to approach a small boy. But it was the only thing he could think of. "My name is Brett. I'm an old friend of your mom's."

His son placed a small hand in his, and a flood of warmth filled Brett's chest as they shook.

It wasn't all that he wanted from their relationship, but it was a start.

"Listen," he said to Kelly. "It was nice talking to you, but I really have to run."

She nodded, and as he rose from his seat, she stood, too. "I'm sure we can work out something. Thanks for understanding."

"I'll do anything I can to make this easy for everyone involved."

"I appreciate that."

"If you have a pen and paper, I'll give you my cell phone number."

She opened a drawer in the lamp table and pulled out a pad and pencil. He gave her all of his contact numbers, including the address where he was staying.

Maybe he ought to think about buying a house of his own, a place where Justin could have a bedroom.

Before leaving, he took one last look at his son, a bright-eyed little boy who didn't know who he was—yet. "It was nice meeting you, Justin. I hope I get to see you again real soon."

For the first time in years, Brett felt a surge of hope.

See what could happen when two people who loved a child put the kid's best interests at heart?

He just wished there was something he could do to make Caitlin see that.

Unless, of course, he was wrong about Zack, and the two of them had nothing in common.

Brett wasn't sure when the idea surfaced. Probably during some of the many catnaps he'd had throughout the night. He'd finally climbed out of bed about four, kicking at the blankets and sheets that had tangled at his feet.

He'd put on a pot of coffee and turned on the TV. But he didn't pay attention to anything on the screen.

Instead, a game plan finally began to form in his mind. And a telephone call to Harry Logan would set that plan in effect. But it was Sunday morning, so he held off until just after seven.

When Kay answered the phone, Brett apologized for calling so early.

"That's not a problem," Kay said. "We've been up for nearly an hour. We're going to the early service this morning."

"Good. Can I please speak to Harry?"

"Sure."

A moment or two later, his friend and mentor answered. "What's up?"

"I'd like to drive out to Riverview Correctional Facility and speak to Zack Henderson."

"Why?"

"Maybe I can talk the guy into giving up his efforts to get custody of Emily."

And if not, then Brett would find out what kind of man Caitlin was up against. Or rather, the kind of man they were both up against, because as much as he wanted to steer clear of domestic turmoil, he wasn't going to be able to. Not any longer.

"Is there anything I need to do to set up a visitation like that?" he asked Harry.

"Let me make a few calls, and I'll get back to you."

Three hours later, Brett drove about a hundred miles east of town to a vast stretch of land that housed convicted criminals until they could pay their debt to society.

He wasn't sure where the name Riverview came into play. Maybe from the dry creek bed that ran through the stretch of sage-dotted desert on which the prison had been built.

After a lengthy security process Harry hadn't even begun to prepare him for, Brett was allowed to see Emily's father in a visiting area.

He wasn't sure what he expected, but not the tall, hulk of a man dressed in a bright orange jumpsuit. Zack Henderson stood about six foot six and had to weigh two hundred and fifty pounds. His dark hair, long and in need of a cut, curled at the shoulders.

Baby blue eyes claimed an innocence the rest of the man didn't have.

"Who are you?" Henderson asked.

"My name is Brett Tanner. I'm a friend and neighbor of the woman who has been raising your daughter."

Those eyes merely studied him. "The social worker told me my little girl's name is Emily. How is she?"

"She's doing great."

For a guy who'd had hours to rehearse his speech, Brett wasn't sure what to say next.

"I'm also a friend of Harry Logan's," he added as a lead-in, as a better introduction. Or maybe he wanted to use it as a validation of their commonality, whatever that might be.

"How is Harry?" Zack asked. "Last I heard he'd had open-heart surgery."

"He's doing great now. Still having barbecues and beach parties."

Zack nodded. "I nearly made it to one of those."

Brett tried to read the look in his eye. Regret that he hadn't taken Harry's advice, his offer of a way out?

The prisoner glanced down at his hands, big hands bearing several scars. "I did my share of trouble-making as a kid, and there were several instances when I deserved charges of delinquency or whatever. But I didn't participate in that damned robbery that landed me here."

"That's what I heard." Brett still wasn't sure

whether he believed the guy, but he figured it wouldn't hurt to accept his story. Especially since he wanted to befriend Zack. Sort of.

"Detective Logan had been after me for some time to attend one of his get-togethers. A beach party. A football game at the park. And I finally gave in and decided to give it a shot."

Harry had mentioned Zack was supposed to attend some informal food and game fest at the Bayside Marina.

"My truck had transmission trouble that day," Zack said. "And about the time I'd decided to forget about going, Ray Montalvo drove up. We'd been friends for years, although Ray's troublemaking spree was more hell-bent than mine. And steering clear of him had been one of Harry's suggestions— a piece of advice I'd taken."

Brett listened to the man's story, wondering if it was just another instance of a jailbird claiming his false innocence.

"I had no idea how big of a mistake I was making when I asked Ray if I could bum a ride with him to the marina." Those blue eyes snagged Brett's, professing honesty. And like Harry had claimed earlier, Brett wanted to believe him, too.

For Emily's sake.

"Ray agreed to drop me off, but he needed to go by the Speedy Stop first. I was out of smokes, so I said, 'no problem.'" Zack scoffed. *"No problem."*

Brett watched as the man's mind took him back five years, back to the scene of the crime.

"After I walked inside, Ray pulled a ski mask out of his pocket and drew a gun. Then he entered and ordered the lady behind the cash register to hand over the money. I'm not sure if there was any kind of buzzer used as an alert, but as she started filling a brown bag with cash from her till, the manager rushed out of the back room with a gun, and shots were fired."

"What did you do?" Brett asked.

"I ran for cover. Ray shot the cashier in the shoulder, and when the manager turned to look at his wounded employee, he was shot in the back. Ray demanded that I get in the friggin' car, but I refused. And he drove off without me." Again, Zack's gaze sought Brett's. "I don't expect you to accept my side of the story. Hell, no one in the D.A.'s office believed that a guy like me, a juvenile delinquent who'd been in trouble more times than not, wasn't involved."

"And so you ended up here," Brett supplied.

"I turned over Ray's name as part of a plea bargain. It's always chapped my hide that I had to spend time for a crime I didn't commit."

Brett imagined it would. "So what's your game plan now?"

"I'm hoping to get out of here and get my life back on track. An old neighbor who'd once taken a liking to me as a youngster offered me work as a heavy equipment operator. And I want to try to make it up to my kid for her having to spend the first four years of her life in foster care." He leaned back in the gray plastic chair. "I plan to be a decent citizen and a good father to my daughter."

"I'm glad to hear it," Brett said. "But have you thought about how difficult it will be for a little girl to leave the only home she's had, to give up the only mother she's ever known?"

"I suppose it'll be tough. But I want to do right by her."

"How about taking things slow and easy?" Brett asked. "Drop the request for complete custody for a while. Maybe start off with visitation until you get to know each other better."

Zack didn't respond right away, so Brett continued. "Caitlin is one of the most loving women I've ever met. She's a hell of a mother to that child, and the only mother Emily has known."

"She wants to adopt her," Zack said. "And I can't let that happen. I don't want to give up my little girl."

"I can understand that. Emily is a beautiful child who would make anyone proud to be her daddy." Even Brett, he realized, his heart crunching at the thought. "But a custody battle and a sudden uprooting wouldn't do her a bit of good."

"You might have a point," Zack said. "My mom died when I was born, and I went to live with my grandmother for a while. But she had to give me up when I was six, and my life went to hell after that."

"Let's set up a visit as soon as you get out. We can talk about a compromise and working things out at that time."

Zack's gaze slammed into him. "How do *you* fit into all of this?"

It seemed odd that his first emotional confession was to a convicted felon in prison. But what the hell. "I'm in love with Caitlin. And if she'll have me, I'd like to marry her."

Zack nodded, as though that made perfect sense.

"And I love your daughter, too," Brett added with a smile. "She's a great kid."

"That's nice to know."

Brett grinned. "But I hope you like cats and dogs. Emily is real big on pets, but her mother—or rather Caitlin—is allergic."

Zack returned his smile. "I don't know much about kids, especially little girls. So I appreciate your insight. And I wouldn't mind having a pet. It might help break the ice between us."

"I'm sure it will." Brett stood and extended a hand to Emily's father, a man willing to put his daughter's best interests first.

"Thanks for driving out here," Zack said.

"I'm glad I did." Brett shook the man's hand. "Good luck."

On the way back to Bayside, he thought about what he'd admitted to Zack.

That he loved Caitlin and wanted to marry her.

It had been the truth. Brett was in this thing for the duration—if she'd have him.

But supporting her was going to be tough, if she didn't agree to a compromise. And not just because Brett wasn't up for a fight.

He'd come to the conclusion that Zack Henderson had been wrongfully accused and imprisoned for a crime he didn't commit. And he admired the man for wanting what was best for his daughter.

But what if Caitlin refused to recognize that?

Chapter Twelve

Caitlin returned home from the hospital on Sunday evening, eager to kick off her shoes and soak in the tub.

It had been an exceptionally brutal afternoon and evening in the E.R.

Along with the standard broken bones that needed to be set and the wounds that needed to be stitched, a head-on collision on I-5 had sent nine people to the hospital, including the drunk driver who'd caused the tragic accident.

From what Caitlin had gathered, the intoxicated young man, convinced he was okay, wrestled the keys away from a buddy and proceeded to drive home against his friends' advice. Just minutes later, he entered the freeway, heading north in the southbound lane and struck a van loaded with tourists on their way to Bucaneer Water Park.

The eight people in the van, members of an extended family, were all seriously injured. Three-year-old Kelsey, who'd been held in her aunt's lap rather than secured in a car seat, suffered a skull fracture.

In order to fit everyone in the van, Kelsey's mother left the car seat in a smaller rental car back at the hotel, when they'd headed out on a short, five-minute drive to the water park. The poor mother, who blamed herself for her daughter's injury, had been inconsolable, especially when she'd learned little Kelsey was unconscious and in critical condition.

The father had received some pretty significant contusions to his head and face, but after he'd been stitched up, he was able to sit at his child's bedside. But the mother, with a broken pelvis and internal bleeding, had been too seriously injured to get out of bed.

When her wails became uncontrollable, jeopardizing her own medical treatment, Luke—Brett's friend, Dr. Wynters—had sedated her.

The maternal cries finally ceased, but that didn't stop Caitlin from empathizing with the woman's pain. She couldn't imagine a worse heartbreak than to lose a child.

By the time Caitlin had clocked out, the pediatric neurosurgeon had decided to operate.

Even though she tried not to become emotionally involved with the patients who moved in and out of her care while she worked in the E.R., Caitlin had asked Luke to call her with an update.

As she trudged from the carport to the walkway, she kneaded her temples, trying to eliminate the tightness that promised a tension headache was on the way, and whispered another prayer for Kelsey's recovery. Then she continued to the Blackstone's door.

While on the porch, she looked across the way to the soft light shining from Brett's living room window.

That was weird. When had she started thinking about the condo as Brett's, rather than Greg's?

She had an urge to give her neighbor a call, to tell him how difficult her day had been and how much her heart ached. To ask for a hug.

But she couldn't do that, no matter how badly she wanted to. Things had changed between them. And although she loved him, his feelings for her didn't run anywhere near as deep.

She lifted her hand to ring the bell, but decided, since it was after eleven and Mary usually turned in early, she should knock lightly instead. But when Scruffy barked like crazy, announcing her arrival, she realized being quiet didn't really matter.

Gerald, who held the squirmy little terrier in his arms, opened the door. "Come on in, Caitlin."

"Thanks."

"Looks like you had a rough night," he said, as he led her to the living room.

Was it obvious just by looking at her? Or had he come to that conclusion because of the time? She supposed it didn't matter.

"Yes, it was. My shift was more difficult than usual." She stretched out the kinks in her neck and shoulders. "I hope Emily behaved for you."

"She was perfect, like always. And just as entertaining." Gerald nodded toward the green tweed sofa, where Emily slept.

"Good." Caitlin never ceased to be amazed at the way Emily was growing, the way her personality was developing. What a daily blessing she had become.

"Let me carry her home for you," her elderly neighbor volunteered.

Caitlin wanted to tell him that it wasn't necessary. She was eager to hold her child close, to breathe in her little-girl scent. To remind herself that Emily was safe and healthy—and not lying on an operating table or in the pediatric I.C.U. But if she carried Emily, she'd have to fumble with the key at her door.

"Thanks, Gerald. I'd appreciate that, if you don't mind."

As they walked to her house, once again she glanced at the muted blue light coming from Brett's living room window. Was he engrossed in a TV show? Dozing on the couch?

And once again, she scolded herself for noticing, for caring. For wishing he loved her, the way she loved him.

She slid the key into the lock and opened her front door.

After she'd put Emily to bed and had seen Gerald out, she filled the bath with hot water, adding lilac bath salts as aromatherapy.

After nights like this, soaking in the tub in a candlelit bathroom helped to relax her body and ease her troubled mind.

As she turned off the faucet, she decided to leave the door ajar, just in case Emily awakened. It didn't happen often, but sometimes, when Caitlin hadn't been the one to kiss Emily good-night and tuck her into bed, she woke up and cried out for her mommy.

And that was still another reason why Caitlin couldn't stand by and let her daughter be placed in the care of her father, a man neither of them knew.

She lit the candle on the counter, and using only the flicker of the flame and the light in the hall to see, she slowly undressed, casting off her clothing much easier than she could her cares. Then she clipped her hair up in a twist and stepped into the tub.

As she'd hoped, the water was hot enough that she had to slowly ease herself into the comforting bath.

She wasn't sure how long she'd soaked, her head against the backrest, one leg extended, one knee bent. But it hadn't been nearly long enough, when a knock sounded at the door.

Who could it be at this hour of the night?

Had Emily forgotten something at Mary and Gerald's?

She climbed from the tub, dried with quick, brisk strokes and slipped on the pink terry cloth robe that hung from a hook on the bathroom door.

When she reached the entry, she peered through the peephole, but couldn't quite make out who was standing on the porch. So she clutched the bulky lapel of her robe and asked, "Who's there?"

"It's me. Brett."

Her heart skipped a beat, and her hand trembled, as she reached for the deadbolt, opened the door and let him in.

He ran a hand through his hair. "I'm sorry if this is a bad time. I know it's late. But I wanted to talk to you, and I didn't want to wait until morning."

"All right." She closed the door behind him.

His hair was a bit scruffy, as though he'd raked his fingers through the strands several times this evening. And he wasn't smiling. But she still found him appealing.

He wore a pair of navy blue sweatpants and a plain white T-shirt—nothing fancy. Just his night-clothes, she supposed. Yet he looked like a worn but dashing swashbuckler to her. One with a dark and dangerous secret.

"Mind if I sit?" he asked.

"Not at all."

She followed him to the sofa and took a seat next to him. Not too close, though.

"I took some of my own advice," he told her.

"What did you do?"

"I went to see Kelly, my ex-wife. And I asked to be a part of my son's life."

She knew how badly he missed his little boy. And she hoped the woman would be agreeable. "How did it go?"

"It might take a little time, since Justin doesn't re-ally know me and believes that her husband is his fa-ther. But she agreed to tell him the truth. She wanted to talk it over with her husband, first. Hopefully, the guy won't change her mind."

"I'm glad that things seem to be working out for you." Caitlin glanced at her lap, saw that her knee had slipped out into the open. She tugged at the edge of her robe to cover herself, although the effort seemed silly, considering his sexual exploration of her body the other night.

The sweet memory continued to assault her, in spite of—or maybe because of—the fact it would never happen again.

He didn't appear to notice her self-consciousness, as he studied the hands that rested on his thighs. Then he looked up, and his gaze sought hers like a drowning man grappling for something floating on the water. "And after I talked to Kelly, I did something else."

His expression seemed to ask for understanding. Or maybe he wanted her support.

"What did you do?" she asked, encouraging him to continue sharing a part of himself and his day with her.

"I drove out to Riverview and visited Zack."

Her heart dropped to her stomach, then rose up to her throat. "Why?"

"You're asking *why,* rather than wanting to know what I found out?"

"Why came to mind first," she said. "And yes. I'd like to know what you learned."

Brett stood, unable to remain seated. He felt too confined by her gaze, by his fear of getting the words out right.

He began to pace the living room, then returned to stand before the sofa on which she sat. The scent of lilac snaked around him, making him want to pull her into his arms. But he refrained. There was a good chance, after she heard what he had to say, that she'd boot him out. Tell him to get lost and never cross her threshold again.

But he had to take the chance.

For Emily.

For her.

And, if they were ever going to have any kind of future together, for them.

"I went out to see him because you've gotten under my skin, even though I've avoided women with kids in the past. And I wanted to meet him because I'd like to help, as long as I can do it on my own terms."

She stood and faced him, with her arms folded across her chest, her sea-green eyes turning stormy. "And just how did you expect to help?"

"I wanted to know what kind of man he used to be, what five years in prison had done to him. I also wanted to know what kind of man he is now. And more importantly, what kind of father he'll be."

Her eyes welled with tears, but she seemed to hold them at bay. "And what did you find out?"

"He'd been an unhappy teenager, like me, who'd rebelled and hooked up with some bad friends. But Harry Logan had spotted something in him, that same something he'd found in me. Zack was heading to the Bayside Marina to meet Harry and the other guys the night of the robbery. Hell, I might have been at the same function, I don't know."

She brushed a loose strand of hair from her cheek with the back of her hand. "But he was arrested for his part in an armed robbery."

"That's true. He caught a ride from Ray Montalvo, a young thug he'd once thought of as a friend. Zack had no idea a robbery was going down."

"You believe that?"

"Yeah, I do. When the gunman drove away, Zack stayed behind. A guilty man wouldn't have done that."

One of the tears she'd been fighting slipped down her cheek, but she made no effort to wipe it away. "If he's convinced you that he's a good person, then he'll probably convince the judge in family court. And then they'll take Emily away from me."

Brett took her by the hand, drew her close. "Not so fast. Zack isn't any more sure of himself as a father than I am. And he wants what's best for his daughter. He's willing to drop the custody issue, at least for the time being, if you'll let him see her."

She pulled back her hand. "How do I know she'll be safe with him?"

"You don't, I suppose. He's a big hulk of a guy, Caitlin. And other than blue eyes, the color of Emily's, he looks formidable. But I have a feeling he'll be a real marshmallow after Emily gets a hold of him." Brett couldn't stifle a grin. "The poor guy will probably end up with a houseful of dogs and cats, if Emily ever brings home a stray and looks up at him with those pretty blue peepers."

Caitlin didn't respond right away, which he figured was a good thing. She had to be thinking about what he'd said, otherwise she would have voiced an argument.

"Zack is going to call me when he gets out," Brett added. "And we can set up a casual meeting, maybe at Harry's place. You'd feel safe there, wouldn't you?"

"I…" She swallowed hard. "I guess so."

"And you could see how he reacts with her. He admitted that he wasn't used to kids, and I think he'd appreciate some coaching."

"They give parenting classes at the Y," she said.

Was she softening? Or refusing to offer the man some guidance?

"Do you hear what I'm saying, Caitlin?"

"Yes. He's not going to try to take her away. Not yet. And he wants to spend time with her, even though he isn't sure how to take care of her."

Brett tilted her chin with the tip of his finger. "He was raised by his grandmother and was only six when he left her care. And according to him, that's when his whole life went to hell. He's very much aware of how important your relationship with Emily is. And I don't think he'll try to take her away. He just wants to build a relationship with her. Surely, you can see that."

Her lips quivered, and her eyes filled again. "It's still going to be hard for me to share her."

"I gotta believe that the more people who love a child, the better."

She nodded, but bit down upon her lip, as though willing it not to tremble.

He slipped an arm around her. "It'll be okay, I promise."

She leaned into his embrace. "How do you know?"

"Maybe because I have faith in Harry's ability to spot the good in a troubled young man. And maybe because I've picked up a bit of that skill myself." He rested his cheek against her hair, savored her lilac scent.

He half expected her to pull away, but she clung to him. So he relished the feel of her in his arms, the way his chest swelled to have her so close.

"And I went to visit him because I'm going to see you through this."

"You are?" She pulled away and gazed into his eyes. "I guess I can't ask for more than that."

What would she say if he leveled with her, if he spilled his guts and told her he loved her, even though he couldn't offer her the kind of family she deserved?

He opened his mouth, but for some dumb reason, the words wouldn't come.

"Thank you," she said, her voice whisper soft.

"For wanting things to work out for all of us?" he asked.

She drew back, her eyes catching his. "What do you mean, for *all* of us?"

How much clearer did he have to be?

He cupped her cheek, his thumbs drawing slow circles on her skin. "I don't know what kind of a future we could have, honey. I'd be away from home more times than not. So I can't provide you with the kind of Norman Rockwell family that you and Emily deserve. But I love you, Caitlin. And I'd marry you in a heartbeat, if I thought that you might someday feel the same way."

Her lips parted, and her eyes brightened, as she raised on tiptoe and wrapped her arms around his neck. "I'm in love with you, too. I was just afraid to tell you."

"Ah, Caitie." He lowered his mouth to hers, kissing her with all the love in his battered heart.

As his tongue swept the inside of her mouth, claiming it as his own, he tasted her, savored her and the love they'd been blessed with.

Their passion soared, as their blood rushed and pheromones surged. The kiss built in intensity, until he was lost in a heady—and oh so healthy—combination of lust and love.

His hands roamed the terry cloth she wore until he felt the sash and tugged on it.

She placed her hands on his chest and slowly broke the kiss. "Let's take this into the bedroom."

"Good idea." Then he stiffened, his memory tossing a bucket of cold water over him. "But we used every last condom."

A wry smile tugged at her lips. "I…uh…was cleaning the bathroom yesterday and found one we missed."

He kissed the tip of her nose. "That's good news. The celebration I was hoping for wouldn't have been the same without the fireworks I plan to set off."

Then he took her by the hand and led her into the bedroom, where she opened the nightstand drawer and pulled out a condom.

"I put it in here," she said. "Near the bed…just in case."

"Good idea. And I have a better one." He slowly pulled the sash, opening the robe and allowing him a glimpse of her sweet body, a vision of what would be his for the rest of his life. "You're beautiful, honey. And I can't believe you're all mine."

"You've got that right, Lieutenant." Then she tugged at the hem of his shirt, lifting it over his head. "And you're all mine."

Her fingers skimmed the expanse of his chest, then she tugged at the waistband of his sweats, letting him know that she wanted him as badly as he wanted her.

It was hard to believe they'd have the rest of their lives to love each other, to create a family. To make babies of their own.

"I love you," he whispered, before kissing her again.

Caitlin opened her mouth for Brett, just as she'd opened her heart. She leaned into his erection, fanning his desire with her own.

A low groan formed in his throat, and he lifted her and carried her to the bed, where he loved her with his hands and with his kisses.

As they lay on top of the goose-down comforter, he hovered over her.

She stroked the light bristles of his beard, studied the passion that deepened the shade of his eyes. "I want you inside of me, where you belong."

"I can't think of any place I'd rather be." Then he brushed a kiss across her brow before reaching for the condom from the top of the nightstand, where she'd left it.

When he'd protected them both, she opened for him. He entered slowly, as if prolonging the thrill of their joining, then thrust forward. She arched up, to take him as deeply as she could.

A loving rhythm built until they reached a mountainous crest that promised a breath-catching view of forever.

As a star-sparkling orgasm shot across her mind's eye, sending her over the edge and setting off a magical climax that made her cry out, he shuddered with his own release.

They lay still for a while, wrapped in the love they'd found in each other's arms, their hearts beating in time.

Caitlin had no idea what the future would bring, either, but she knew they could weather any storm, as long as she and Brett had each other.

Caitlin slept like a dream and, when she woke, the blanket pulled up to her chin, her back tucked lovingly against Brett's chest, she was greeted by the sound of Emily's giggle.

Uh-oh. They'd been caught.

Well, if Brett was going to be her husband and Emily's father, they'd better get used to being interrupted. And they'd have to remember to put on some clothes after making love.

She opened her eyes, to find she'd been the only one in the small house sleeping.

"Okay," Brett said to Emily. "Now that the pretty sleepyhead is awake, we can talk louder."

"Is it really true?" Emily asked. "Is Brett going to marry us?"

Caitlin glanced over her shoulder, at the man she loved.

He shrugged, then shot her a crooked grin. "I didn't want her to think this was just a fluke or a sleepover."

She supposed he was right. They may as well break the news now. "Yes, honey. And from what Brett told me several different times last night, he wants to marry us as soon as possible."

Emily clapped her hands and jumped up and down. "Goodie. Do I get to be the flower girl?"

"Of course," she said, unable to hide a smile that had burst from her heart. Had those two already started planning the wedding? "You can even be my maid of honor, if you'd like."

"Which one of the Barbie dolls is that?" Emily asked.

Caitlin laughed. "I think it's Midge. But either way, you'll be the most important member of the wedding party."

Brett, who had propped himself up on an elbow, chuckled. "It looks like you two ladies will have to go shopping, while I make sure I won't get deployed before the honeymoon."

"Do you think that will happen?" Caitlin asked, pressing the edge of the sheet against her chest, so that it continued to cover her breasts.

"Probably not that soon. But will you be okay when it does?"

"Of course." She understood the sacrifices made by military families. And she'd do her part by keeping the home fires burning. "But I'd like you to be around for a while, so I can enjoy being your wife."

"I think I've got a couple of months."

"Good. Then let's set a date for the ceremony so we don't waste any time together."

"You don't have to ask me twice. I was ready to marry you last night." He ran a protective hand along the sheet-covered curve of her hip. "But if you don't mind, I'd like to go to the hardware store before we apply for a license."

"Okay." She scrunched her face. "But what do you plan to get there?"

"I need to get some lumber, wire, hammers, nails. On second thought, I'd better make a list. Emily and I have to build a cathouse."

Emily's eyes widened. "A cathouse?"

"Well, sure. If I'm moving in here with you, I can't leave the cats alone at Greg's. And since they can't live inside your mommy's house, they'll need their own place on the patio."

"I think a cattery is the right term," Caitlin said with a smile.

"Can your allergies handle having the cats on the patio?" he asked.

"I'm sure, with an occasional antihistamine, I'll be all right."

"Mommy, after breakfast, can I go and tell Gerald and Mary that I'm going to have a daddy?"

Emily was going to have two fathers, but Caitlin

would wait to explain that. "Of course, you can tell them. Why don't you get dressed and brush your teeth. We'll meet you in the kitchen for breakfast."

"Okay."

As the child dashed out of the bedroom, Caitlin turned in bed, so she could face Brett. "I guess we'd better tell her about Zack, although I'm not looking forward to it."

"We'll tell her she's going to be a lucky little girl, since she'll have two daddies who love her."

"Do you really think she's going to be lucky?" Caitlin asked, hoping yet not convinced that would be the case.

"I think she'll be very fortunate—as long as we keep a positive attitude and work along with Zack."

"You know something?" Caitlin brushed a kiss across his brow. "I feel pretty fortunate, too."

Brett grinned from ear to ear. "Me, too." Then he gave her a long, lingering kiss.

When Caitlin climbed from bed and picked up the robe that lay on the floor where they'd discarded it, Brett placed his hands under his head and considered the changes a marriage to Caitlin would make in his life.

For years, he'd sworn that he would never be a part of a broken family again, but that was before Caitlin and Emily had touched his heart.

As he threw off the sheets and caught a whiff of lilac mingled with the scent of their lovemaking, he realized something. This family wasn't broken. It was coming together rather nicely, joining half siblings, parents and stepparents.

And as long as Caitlin loved him, the future didn't scare him a bit.

Of course, there was a lot they had to leave up to Kelly and Zack.

Chapter Thirteen

A week later, just days before the small, intimate wedding Brett and Caitlin planned to have in the Logans' backyard, Zack Henderson was released from prison. And one of his first calls from the outside was to Brett.

Caitlin might have been more stressed about what his release and freedom might bring had she not known the comfort and strength of Brett's love. His optimism helped her maintain an emotional balance and nurture a hope that the man wouldn't upset their lives too much.

But as they got ready to meet with Zack for the first time, she was still nervous. And still worried about the motives of the man who wanted to be a part of Emily's life.

"Are you ready?" Brett asked from a chair in the living room.

"Just about." Caitlin plaited a small strand of Emily's hair into a braid with stiff, uncooperative fingers, then held the ends together with a red kitty-cat barrette.

"Do you think my daddy is going to like me?" Emily asked.

"Of course, sweetheart," Caitlin said, not wanting her daughter to experience any of the stress she was going through. "He's going to love you."

"But how come he never came to my house before?"

Caitlin tried hard to wrestle her own concerns and hide them from her expression. "He would have, honey. But he wasn't able to."

"Why not?"

Caitlin hated to tell her he'd been in prison. So she searched for a vague answer. "He lived far away from town and wasn't able to travel."

She glanced in the mirror and spotted Emily's furrowed brow. Obviously, her daughter wasn't content with the explanation.

"Come on, sweetie. Brett's waiting for us." Caitlin put the hairbrush and comb in the drawer, then checked her own appearance one more time.

Emily tugged at the hem of Caitlin's green cotton blouse. "But I thought Brett was going to be my daddy."

This was so confusing for the child.

"You're lucky. You get to have two daddies."

"Am I s'posed to call them both Daddy?"

In spite of Brett's positive outlook, Caitlin was afraid the whole meeting would blow up in their faces. "You can call them by their names, if it makes it easy for you today."

"You mean call them Brett and Zack?" Emily seemed to think about that for a while, as Caitlin led her into the living room, where Brett waited.

As far as she was concerned, she wanted Brett to be Emily's only daddy. Her *real* daddy. But that wasn't possible.

"You girls look pretty." Brett smiled broadly and walked them to the door. He stopped at the threshold, long enough to give Caitlin a hug and whisper softly, "Everything is going to work out fine."

She nodded, appreciating his words, even if they didn't ease her apprehension.

The ride to the Logans' was uneventful and quiet, other than Emily's chatter about how much the cats liked the new cat house, with its built-in, carpeted climbing structure that practically took up the entire patio.

"I think we'd better call it a cattery," Caitlin reminded them both again.

Before long, they pulled in front of the Logans' two-story, Cape Cod-style house on Bayside Drive. Brett parked the Expedition, then helped Emily from the back seat.

"Is my daddy here yet?" Emily asked.

"I'm not sure." Brett studied the vintage Camaro parked at the curb. "This could be his car."

The color was a combination of age-faded black and primer gray. But it was clean, and the tires looked new.

As they made their way to the door, a floral welcome mat awaited them on the porch.

Brett slid Caitlin a smile, then rang the bell.

Moments later, Kay answered. She gave them each a hug, then invited them into her living room, where a big man sat upon the sofa. A dimpled smile softened a dark and dangerous edge.

He was a handsome man, Caitlin decided.

His black hair nearly reached his shoulders, but it was clean and neat. He stood when they entered, and Brett extended a hand in greeting.

Brett was six feet tall, but he was almost dwarfed by Zack. Wow. Emily's father was enormous. And buff. He must have worked out a lot in the prison gym.

"You're as big as the Jack in the Beanstalk giant," Emily told him, clearly in awe of her father, although not appearing frightened.

The man squatted to be on a more equal level with the child. He smiled, pretty sky-blue eyes, just like Emily's, glimmering. "Nah. That guy was a lot bigger than me. And kind of mean, wasn't he?"

She nodded. "But you're not mean, huh, Daddy."

Zack looked as though she could have blown him over with an eyelash flutter. "No, I'm not mean. Especially not to little girls."

Her eyes widened, and she crossed her arms, as though inspecting him. "Who are you mean to?"

Zack looked up at Brett, then at Caitlin, as if trying to get some help with his response, but he was

on his own. And the fact that he looked a bit sheepish with Emily made Caitlin feel a lot better.

"I'm not mean to anyone."

"Then you're a good giant." She placed a hand on
his knee, and he merely looked at it, as though mar-
veling at the contrast of the soft little hand on rugged black denim.

"I'm not used to little girls, so you'll have to tell
me all about the things they like to do. Like what kind
of TV shows they like to watch and the food they like
to eat."

Emily smiled. "That's easy. Little girls like Hello
Kitty cartoons and pizza and Barbies and pink ice
cream and party shoes that are shiny and new." She
glanced at the floor and lifted her foot, showing him
the shoes Caitlin had purchased last week. "See?
Like these."

"They're very pretty," Zack said, with a grin. "It
sounds like I've got a lot to learn."

"That's okay. I can help you, Daddy."

When he glanced up, Caitlin could have sworn she
saw a tear glisten in his eye.

"Daddy," Emily said, drawing the man's rapt attention. "Can I ask you a question?"

"Sure."

"How come you never came to see me before?
Mommy said you lived far away. But you didn't even
call me on the telephone, and Mommy does that even
when she's busy at work."

Zack looked as though he'd been roped and left hog-
tied, but he placed his hand softly on hers. "I was in jail."

"With the bad guys?" she asked. "Were you the policeman who had to catch them all?"

Caitlin was as anxious as Emily was for a response. Sometimes, it was difficult giving her precocious daughter a truthful, yet age-appropriate answer to her questions.

Zack paused momentarily, as if trying to come up with a response that might satisfy her. "I'm going to make you a promise, Emily. I'm always going to tell you the truth." Then he began his explanation. "Right before you were born, I made a mistake and rode in a bad guy's car. He used to be a friend of mine, but I learned the hard way that he wasn't the kind of friend I should trust. And when he did something wrong, I had to go to jail, too."

She placed her free hand on his cheek. "I'm sorry, Daddy. That's too bad. Are you all done at jail?"

"Yes. And that's another promise I'll make you. I won't ever go back there again."

The fact that Zack had answered his daughter honestly touched Caitlin's heart, and she couldn't help believing his story. And his promise.

Because he'd leveled with Emily, and she'd accepted it so well, Caitlin realized she'd have to be honest, too. She'd have to tell Emily the truth about being a foster child.

Hopefully, as long as Caitlin reaffirmed her love, and because of the bond they had, her daughter would handle that news just as well as she had Zack's.

"Well, now that you've all met and had a chance

to chat," Kay said, "can I offer anyone a slice of birthday cake and a scoop of ice cream?"

"Whose birthday is it?" Emily asked.

"Since you and your daddy have missed so many birthdays, I thought it might be nice if we celebrated all of them this afternoon."

Until that moment, Caitlin hadn't realized how special Harry and his wife were, how thoughtful and supportive. And she decided, then and there, that she was happy to be a part of the Logans' extended family.

"Emily, why don't you come help me put the candles on the cake," the older woman said, as she took the little girl by the hand, leaving the adults a moment to speak among themselves.

Zack stood, then brushed his hands against his black denim-clad thighs. "I can't get over what a sweet little girl she is. You've obviously done a great job raising her."

"Thanks," Caitlin said. "She's been an absolute joy and a pleasure to have."

Then she kicked herself for leaving an opening for him to thank her and say he'd be taking over from now on. But just as his honesty with Emily had taken her by surprise, so did his response.

"I want to do right by her and to be a dad she can be proud of. But to tell you the truth, it's a bit scary and overwhelming for a guy who had a lousy upbringing. So I hope you'll bear with me."

"Caitlin is a whiz at being a mother and with all the family stuff," Brett said. "I'm in kind of the same boat you're in. Being a father is pretty new. And I don't want to screw up, either."

"From what I understand," Caitlin said, her gaze lighting on the retired detective, "you both have a perfectly good role model in Harry."

The older man smiled, clearly pleased with the compliment. "Both of you guys will do a great job fathering that little girl."

Before anyone could comment, Kay and Emily carried in the birthday cake with four flickering candles.

"We don't have presents," Emily explained, "'cause being a family is the best gift of all."

Caitlin, with her heart swelling to the point of overflowing, agreed. "You've got that right, Em. We've all been blessed."

And God willing, Brett's son, Justin, would join them soon.

On Saturday morning, the day of the wedding, Brett and Caitlin were just getting ready to head out the door when the telephone rang.

"I'll get it," Emily said, as she dashed through the house, her party shoes tapping on the hardwood floor.

She picked up the receiver and answered the phone. "Hello?"

Brett chuckled. Girls and telephones. It started early, he supposed.

"Yes. Here he is." She handed him the phone. "It's a lady. And she wants to talk to you."

"Hello," he answered, eager to hang up and be on their way.

"It's me. Kelly."

His heart nearly dropped to the floor. "Is everything all right?"

"Yes, it's fine. I just wanted to let you know that we spoke to Justin. We told him that David loved him more than anything in the world, but that he had another dad. A dad who wanted to visit him."

Brett gripped the phone so tight, his knuckles ached. "Is he all right with it?"

"I think so. He was hurt that we hadn't told him sooner. But other than that, I think he's handling it okay. He'd like to see you."

Brett closed his eyes, relishing the sound of her words.

His son wanted to meet him, too.

Caitlin stepped out of the bathroom and into the living room. She probably wondered what he was doing, chatting on the phone, when he'd been eagerly prodding her and Emily to get dressed so they could leave.

He'd have to explain later. "How's David doing?"

"David?" Kelly paused, as though the question had taken her aback. "He's doing all right. But I think sharing Justin will be hard for him."

"I'll do my best not to step on his toes, Kelly. I meant what I said about putting Justin's best interests first." Brett glanced at Caitlin. Her smile told him she understood the importance of the call.

"I appreciate your attitude," Kelly said. "Maybe Justin will come out the better because of this."

"That's my intention. And I'll do everything in my

power to make sure this is a positive experience for all of us." Again, his gaze sought Caitlin, and his heart soared, as the pieces of his life began to fall in place. "I'm getting married today—to a wonderful woman I'm sure you'll like. And in a few days, when things get settled, I'll give you a call. Maybe we can have you, Justin and David over for dinner."

"I…uh…sure. That would be nice."

"And Kelly?"

"Yes."

"Thank you for being such a great mother to my son. I doubt he could have handpicked someone better."

"You're…welcome."

"I'll give you a call in a couple of days."

When the line disconnected, Brett turned to Caitlin.

She gave him a hug. "It's amazing what love and compromise can do."

"That's what Harry told me. And he was right." He brushed a kiss upon her hair. "Come on. I'm in a hurry to start the happy ever after part of this thing."

"Me, too!" Emily said. "Just like in my *Fairytale Princess* book."

"Yeah," Brett said, taking his daughter by the hand. "I don't want your mommy kissing any more toads."

Then they drove off into what promised to be a beautiful sunset.

The wedding was small, by most people's stand-ards, with only the Logans, the Blackstones, a couple of neighbors, two nurses from Oceana General and three of Brett's Navy buddies in attendance. Greg, whose flight was due in anytime, was going to try and take a cab from Lindberg field, even if he came late.

Caitlin had asked Luke Wynters to come, too, but he had to work. He did mention that Kelsey, the three-year-old accident victim, was doing much better than anyone had expected, and that the neurosurgeon expected a full recovery. Then he wished her and Brett all the best, saying he couldn't imagine a better or more special setting for a wedding than Harry's parklike backyard.

And she had to agree.

The yard wasn't large, but it was lush and green, with palms and ferns and flowering plants that lined a wrought iron fence that provided a view of the bay.

Tiki lights and candles lit the lawn, where a rented flower-adorned gazebo awaited the bride and groom.

Earlier, they'd been introduced to Reverend Morton, the pastor of Kay's church. The man was pretty down to earth, as far as ministers went. Several times before the ceremony, he'd revealed a sense of humor and a pleasant laugh.

A knock sounded at the guest room door.

"It's me," Kay said, as she peered into the room. "Are you ladies ready?"

"Yes, we are. Please come in."

Kay stepped inside, her eyes sweeping over both Emily and Caitlin, who'd dressed in a simple but elegant white gown. "You're both absolutely beautiful."

"Thank you."

"If you're ready, it's time to walk down the aisle."

Caitlin glanced at her daughter, who looked like a princess in a long, pink satin dress with a matching bow in her hair, and smiled. "We certainly are ready. Aren't we, Em?"

The little girl nodded, her eyes glistening with excitement.

"Then it's time that we get started." Kay led the way through the house and to the side door, where they would travel along the walk to the backyard.

There, they met Harry, who would walk the bride down the aisle.

A harpist, someone Kay knew from her church, was playing a lovely melody. When the silver-haired woman spotted Caitlin, she masterfully altered the chords to begin the wedding march.

Kay handed Emily the basket of rose petals, then prompted the little girl to start down the white cloth-covered aisle to the gazebo where her daddy Brett waited.

As Caitlin drew near, her eyes never left those of her lover, her soon-to-be husband and friend. The man who'd made her life complete.

As Reverend Morton joined them in holy matrimony, making them one, a family that had only begun, Caitlin's heart beat strong and clear. And as the minister introduced Lieutenant and Mrs. Brett Tanner and their daughter, Emily, the beautiful flower girl tugged on his vestment robe.

Her sweet whisper could be heard across the yard,

as she told Reverend Morton, "I have two daddies, now. And that makes me the luckiest girl in the world."

And she was right.

Brett picked her up in his arms, then placed a lingering kiss on Caitlin's lips. "We're all pretty darn lucky."

When the kiss ended, and as the crowd broke into applause, Emily clapped her hands. "And we all get to live happily ever after."

"That's the plan, sweetheart."

Then Lieutenant and Mrs. Tanner, along with their bright-eyed daughter, joined hands and walked down the aisle, eager to begin their life together.

Epilogue

In late summer, Brett and Caitlin sat on an old bed-spread on the sand and watched the sun set over the Pacific, while Justin helped Emily build a castle that would reach the sky.

It was both a sad and happy occasion. They'd just learned that Caitlin was going to have a baby. And that Brett would be shipping out at the beginning of September.

"Here comes another wave," Justin yelled, as he scurried to strengthen the wall he'd built to protect the sand tower.

It did Brett's heart good to see the kids play so well together. They squabbled sometimes, too, like other siblings, he supposed. But it was clear that they cared about each other.

Still, things remained a bit awkward between him and his son. In part, because Brett tried so damn hard not to push himself on the boy and not to step on David's toes. But he had to admit their relationship was getting a little better as time went on, so he couldn't ask for more than that.

"Think I ought to start the fire?" he asked Caitlin.

"Sure. The kids are probably hungry."

As he stacked the wood into the concrete-rimmed pit and wadded up old newspapers, Justin looked up at him. "Hey, Brett. Can I help you?"

"You bet, as long as you remember not to play with matches when an adult isn't around."

"I know. The Bayside Fire Department came to our school and talked to us about that. And one kid, the new boy, Bobby Davenport, is a junior fire marshall."

"Hey," Brett told his son. "I know Bobby's dad. And there's a good chance you'll meet him at the park next weekend. Mr. and Mrs. Logan have planned a big whiffle ball championship."

"Cool."

Brett handed Justin the box of matches and watched as he carefully struck one against the side. It took about three tries and some careful maneuvering to block the breeze, but the flame finally caught.

Justin looked at him, then nibbled on his lip. "Can I ask you something?"

"Shoot."

"I know that you're my dad and all. And that I probably shouldn't call you Brett, like I've been doing."

"I'm okay with it, if you are." Brett didn't want to

make the kid uncomfortable by forcing affection he'd yet to feel.

"Yeah, well it's kind of weird calling you Dad, since my dad, or David... Well, you know what I mean."

"I know just what you mean."

"But you're still my *real* dad."

The acknowledgement touched him, even though his son was having a hard time calling him Dad.

Brett placed a hand on the boy's head, felt the strands that were loaded by a dunk in the ocean and a splatter of sand. "I'm glad David has been such a special man in your life. And he's the only dad you've had for a very long time. I understand. Really."

"Yeah, well I was reading this book the other day. And the boy in it called his stepfather Pop. I know you're not my stepfather, but maybe I could call you that. I think Pop is better than Brett, 'cause that makes you sound like just a friend or a brother or something."

Brett had to blink back the moisture that gathered in his eyes. "I'd love to be called Pop. It sounds perfect."

A smile burst on Justin's face. "Yeah, that's what I was thinking. And it makes you sound more like a *real* dad."

"Oh, no!" Emily shrieked. "Hurry up, Justin. The wave is getting us!"

"Uh-oh. Gotta go." Then he hurried to help his sister.

Caitlin, who'd been watching, eased closer. "What was that all about?"

Brett couldn't hide the emotion any longer, and he

wasn't sure if he even wanted to. They were a family, for cripes sake. And families were allowed to share their feelings.

He swiped at the tears with the back of his hand and grinned at his wife. "Justin's going to call me Pop."

A smile broke out on Caitlin's pretty face, and she drew him into a hug. "That's the best news we've had all day."

"No," Brett said. "Not the best. That little pink dot on the pregnancy test was the best. But this comes in as a close second."

Later, as the kids munched on hot dogs, watermelon slices and potato salad, Brett took his wife's hand and gave it a squeeze. "It's going to be tough when I have to leave all of this."

"I know. It'll be tough on us, too." She placed a kiss on his cheek and nuzzled closer. "But it's your job. It's what you do. And you can rest assured, I'll keep the home fires burning while you're gone."

"I have no doubt about that."

A man couldn't ask for a better wife than Caitlin. And when he shipped out, his job would be even more important than it had been in the past.

Because now he had a family worth fighting for.

* * * * *

Don't miss the next
BAYSIDE BACHELORS *story!*
THE MATCHMAKERS' DADDY (SE#1689)
by Judy Duarte
Available June 2005!
Turn the page for a sneak preview.

Chapter One

Zack Henderson was used to neighbor kids gawking at him when he ran a bulldozer at local construction sites, but usually those kids were boys.

What possible interest could girls have in tractors, dirt and diesel fuel?

Along the block wall that separated the backyards of an older neighborhood from the future site of a new subdivision, the two little girls perched in the summer sun, giggling, whispering to themselves and occasionally waving at him.

And for some goofy reason, he would always wave back. Maybe because it made him feel a bit heroic, in spite of being anything but.

He wiped his hand across his forehead, drying the

perspiration that gathered. Then he took a swig of water from the jug he kept in the cab of his dozer.

God, it was hot today. He glanced at the girls and wondered when they'd get tired or bored and go inside. Not anytime soon, he guessed. The heat and noise didn't seem to bother them at all.

They were sure cute kids. But their interest in him and his tractor had him stumped. What did an ex-con like him know about kids—especially girls? He'd met Emily, his four-year-old daughter, for the very first time a couple of months ago, just after he'd been paroled. And he still felt way out of his league. But he *had* learned Emily was big on kitties and new party shoes—not tractors, dust and noise.

The warm, pungent smell of diesel and the roar of the engine hung in the cab of the D9L Caterpillar, as Zack continued to clear and grub the thirty-seven acres that would soon be a new housing development called Mariposa Glen.

Bob Adams, the owner of Bayside Construction, had taken a chance and hired Zack right out of prison, going so far as to write letters to the parole board on his behalf. Bob's faith in him had been one of the first breaks Zack had received since being convicted of a crime he'd witnessed, but hadn't committed.

Zack swiped at his brow again. After lunch—about the time the girls had taken an interest in his work—he'd shed his shirt. But the heat of the summer sun hadn't eased up, even though it was nearing five.

As he turned the dozer, he again looked at the wall where the children sat. The blonde lifted the hand that rested near the beverage glass, but before he could nod or acknowledge her, the little brown-haired girl reached to take a drink while juggling her teddy bear. The stuffed animal slipped from her grasp, and as she tried to catch it, she lost her balance and tumbled forward.

Damn. That was a long, hard fall for a little kid. He quickly decelerated, threw the gear into Neutral, lowered the dozer blade, then jumped from the rig and ran toward the crying child, who lay on the ground in a heap of pink and white.

His heart pounded in his chest as he leaped over clods of dirt and twigs that had yet to be cleared.

The older girl tried to scramble off the wall, but was having a difficult time of it.

When he reached the girl in the dirt, he knelt by her side. "Are you all right?"

"No," she shrieked between sobs. "I broke my leg. And my back. And my bottom. And it hurts *really* bad."

The crazy kid could have broken her neck. As she sat up and peered at the knee that sported a blood-tinged scrape, she let out a piercing wail.

"I'll go get Mommy's doctor book," the older girl said, as she turned and tried to figure out how to scale the six-foot wall.

"Why don't you go get your mommy instead," Zack suggested. He could use some backup. Surely the child's mother could handle this situation a hell of a lot better than he could. For Pete's sake, he'd never felt so inept in all his life.

"Our mom is at work," the older girl said.

"And what about your dad?" he asked her.

"He's in Heaven."

Oops. What was he supposed to say to that?

Hoping to distract the crying child from her pain and get her thoughts off the death of her father, he asked her name.

She sniffled, sucking back her tears in a ragged wheeze. "J-Jessie."

"It's Jessica Marie," the older girl supplied. "Jessie is her nickname. My name is Becky. I'm named after my grandmother, Rebecca Ann. She's in Heaven, too."

Zack didn't want to touch the Heaven stuff with a ten-foot pole, so he clamped his mouth shut.

"What's *your* name?" Becky asked.

He really didn't want to get chummy with a couple of kids. But he didn't want to be rude, either. "You can call me Zack." He didn't give her a last name; he didn't see a point.

"Our mom's name is Diana," she added. "She's very pretty. And she's nice, too."

He knew for a fact that some pretty mothers left their children alone. But he didn't think *nice* ones would. "Who's looking after you?"

"Megan," Becky supplied. "Our babysitter. She's a teenager."

Thank goodness there was someone better qualified for this than him, even if his successor was in her teens.

The injured child—Jessie—had finally stopped

crying, but the tears had left a telltale muddy path along her cheeks.

"Do you think you can stand up?" he asked her.

She shrugged. "I don't know. But I'll try."

"Good. I'll help you. Then we can go find Megan."

As he tried to pull the little girl to her feet, she cried out. "Owie. I can't. My leg is still broken."

It looked okay to him. Just a little red near the knee.

Oh what the hell. He'd just have to carry her home. Zack glanced at the dozer that sat idling in the field. The crew was spread a little thin this week, so he was the only one working on this project for the next couple of days. But he figured it would be okay to leave the site for a few minutes.

He picked up the teddy bear and handed it to Becky, then scooped Jessie into his arms.

"You sure are strong," Becky said, as she walked along beside him.

He shrugged. Jessie didn't weigh much more than his daughter, but he figured Becky was actually referring to his size more than anything.

At six foot six and with the bulk he'd built up in the prison gym, Zack got plenty of notice on the street. And not just from kids.

"Your muscles are really big," the smaller girl said. "Just like the 'credible Hulk. Do you get green and big when you get mad?"

A smile tugged at his lips. "I get a little red in the face and puff out my chest. But I pretty much stay this color and size."

They walked along the block wall until they reached the end of it, then cut through an unfenced backyard to the street.

"Which house is yours?" he asked, eager to pass the baton—or rather the child—to the sitter.

Becky pointed ahead. "Our house is the white one with the yellow sunflower on the mailbox. My mom painted it. She's a good artist."

As Zack continued down the street in the direction Becky had indicated, she asked, "Are you married?"

It seemed like an odd question, but he answered truthfully. "No, I'm not."

"That's good."

Uh-oh. Warning bells went off in Zack's head, although he wasn't sure why. Surely the preteen didn't have a crush on him. How was a guy supposed to deal with stuff like that?

"Our mom's not married, either," Becky added.

Their mom? Oh, the widow.

He wasn't sure how that came up. But good. Maybe the childish crush thing was the wrong assumption.

"What about you?" he countered. "Are either of you married?"

They both giggled.

Jessie, who no longer appeared to be shaken by her fall, brightened and her brown eyes sparkled. "No, silly. We're just kids."

As Becky lagged behind, Zack turned and noticed she was struggling to keep up with his stride, so he slowed down. He had to do that when walking with Emily, too.

When the girl finally caught up to him, she asked, "Do tractor drivers make a lot of money?"

What kind of question was that? He was making union scale, a good wage, especially for a felon. And he'd be able to buy his own house someday. A place with a second bedroom he could fix up for his daughter and a backyard big enough to hold a swing set, a playhouse and all the other outdoor, childhood necessities he'd yet to learn about.

"I'm happy with my paycheck," he told the girl.

"That's good."

He snuck a glance at Becky's bright-eyed, freckled face and saw the wheels turning. For the life of him, he couldn't figure out what she had on her mind.

But maybe it was only his imagination. He'd never quite gotten a handle on the way women thought. So what made him think a preteen girl would be any less complex?

As they neared the children's house, the child in his arms pointed to an old green Plymouth that rumbled down the street. "Look! Mommy's home."

The Plymouth stopped in the middle of the street, and a slender brunette climbed from the idling car. "What's going on? Jessie, what's the matter?"

"I broke my leg," the girl began, reciting the list of injuries she'd self-diagnosed.

"And this is Zack," her older sister said. "He was driving a tractor in the field and saved her life. Isn't he nice?"

"Yeah," Jessie said. "And Mommy, he's super-strong, too. You should feel his muscles."

The pretty mother flushed and tucked a strand of honey-brown hair behind her ear. She flashed Zack an appreciative smile. "Thank you for helping Jessie. But I'm not sure what she was doing out in the field, since the girls aren't allowed out of the yard while I'm gone."

"We *weren't* in the field," Becky explained. "We were sitting on the wall, watching Zack work. Then Jessie fell over like Humpty Dumpty."

"And Zack put me together again." Jessie patted him on the shoulder.

A bare shoulder, he realized. But heck, he hadn't had time to think about putting on a shirt. Or cleaning up so that he could make a good impression on a woman who seemed to grow lovelier by the minute.

The attractive mother blessed Zack with another sweet smile, and his heart skipped a beat.

"Thank you for rescuing Jessie," she told him, before addressing her oldest daughter. "Becky, where's Megan?"

"She's sick with a major headache and taking a nap on the sofa. But don't worry. I took good care of Jessie."

Zack couldn't help but arch a brow at that comment, but she *had* tried to look after her sister—after the fall.

"We'll talk about that later," the mother said.

"Do you want me to carry her inside for you?" Zack asked, surprised that he'd uttered the words. But as crazy as it seemed, he almost wished she'd say yes.

"Thanks, but I can manage." She lifted her arms to take her daughter from him.

As they tried to shift the girl from one pair of arms to the other, Zack feared he'd get the pretty mother's light blue blouse or her beige slacks dirty. "Be careful. I'm pretty grimy and sweaty."

"That's all right." Her hand brushed his several times, making his skin tingle. But they managed to transfer the child. "I've got her. Thanks."

For a moment their gazes locked, and something sweet and gentle drew him to her, threatening to leave him tongue-tied and stammering.

Of course, he couldn't very well stand there staring at her, especially in front of her daughters so he shook off the mushy feeling. "Well, I'd better go."

Her green eyes glimmered as she nodded, but her gaze never left him. He couldn't help wondering if she found him attractive.

But how stupid was that? She was probably trying to determine his character. And with his luck, her maternal instinct would probably snitch, telling her that he'd spent the past five years in prison.

"Thanks again," she said, giving him his cue, his excuse to cut out and return to work.

"You're welcome."

From behind, he could hear the mother tell the girls to stay off the fence. And that she needed to have a talk with Megan.

What had the girls said their mother's name was? Diana?

He supposed it didn't matter. He doubted he'd ever see her or the girls again.

Still, he couldn't help thinking that she was too

young to be a widow. His thoughts drifted to her late husband. Dying wasn't anything a man looked forward to, that's for sure. But leaving a wife like her behind would make it a whole lot worse.

He struggled with the urge to turn his head, to take one last look at the woman whose daughter had told the truth when she'd said her mom was pretty and nice.

But he didn't.

Women like that didn't give men like him a second glance.

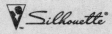

This June

Silhouette®

SPECIAL EDITION™

Presents the exciting finale
of the continuity

MONTANA MAVERICKS

GOLD RUSH GROOMS

Lucky in love—and striking it rich—
beneath the big skies of Montana!

MILLION-DOLLAR MAKEOVER
by Cheryl St.John

In the ultimate rags-to-riches story, plain-Jane Lisa Martin
learns that she's inherited the Queen of Hearts gold mine.
Yet the idea of being rich and powerful is foreign to the
quiet, bookish young woman. So when handsome
Riley Douglas offers to join her payroll and manage the
property, Lisa is grateful. But is Riley too good to be true?

Available in June 2005 at your favorite retail outlet.

Silhouette®

Where love comes alive™

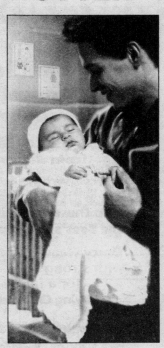

If you enjoyed what you just read,
then we've got an offer you can't resist!

Take 2 bestselling love stories FREE!
Plus get a FREE surprise gift!